SEASIDE FRIENDS

NELLIE BROOKS

Merpaper Press LLC

Copyright © 2022 by Nellie Brooks. All rights reserved.

This is a work of fiction. Names, characters, and places are products of the author's imagination. Any resemblance to actual persons, living or dead, events or locales is entirely coincidental. Any references to historical events, real people, or real places are used fictitiously.

All rights reserved. No part of this publication may be reproduced, distributed, or transmitted in any form or by any means, including photocopying, recording, or other electronic or mechanical methods, without the prior written permission of the publisher, except in the case of brief quotations embodied in critical reviews and certain other noncommercial uses permitted by copyright law. For permission requests, contact the publisher at MerpaperPressLLC@gmail.com.

Edited and proofread by *Karen Meeus Editing, Eagle Eye Proofreading, and Michele Wood Editing.*

Published by Merpaper Press LLC

ISBN-13: 978-1-958957-00-4

Contents

Before

The tide was going out, and the glassy waves left the sand just wet enough for the noon sun to bake it hard. Mela set the Barbie Bubble Bath down and ran to the sea, filling her bucket and running back to pour water into the pink plastic tub.

"My Barbie can take a bath first, and then yours can take one," Amelie said and started to tug the tight, ruffled wedding dress off her smiling doll.

Mela nodded. Amelie had already allowed her to carry the bath and fill it, so it was only fair her friend got the first turn bathing her Barbie. Mela sat beside Amelie on the ground, not caring whether her shorts got wet or sandy. She was wearing a swimsuit under her clothes anyway, like any kid spending the summer in Bay Harbor. Though she and Amelie lived here all the time.

Well, sometimes they were somewhere else, like last week when they'd gone to Sandville to watch the E.T. movie.

Mela felt her insides quiet down. "The movie was so sad," she whispered, knowing what would happen.

Amelie immediately stopped swooshing her Barbie back and forth in the water and looked up. "So sad," she agreed, and her brown eyes started to water. "The poor thing."

Mela wanted to cry too. "It was bodacious," she said, her voice wavering.

A big tear rolled down Amelie's cheek. "It *was* bodacious." She wiped her cheek and studied the wet smear on the back of her hand. "Look." She held out her hand.

Mela nodded. "I know. It makes me cry too."

"But you're not."

Mela looked up into the blue sky. Sometimes the sun made her eyes water. "So what do we say when a movie's bad?" She stood and wiggled out of her wet shorts, then pulled the T-shirt off and tossed it on top.

"I don't know. But if it's good, you can also say gnarly," Amelie said and followed Mela's example. Her pile of clothes looked almost like Mela's; only Amelie's shorts had cool heart stickers on the pockets, while Mela's did not.

Amelie had a dad, and they were rich. Mela didn't have a daddy and wasn't rich. Amelie also had brown eyes and Mela blue ones, but otherwise, they were the same. Even their names were almost the same. They both had m-e-l, which even the kids at school admitted was pretty much proof they belonged together.

"First one in the water wins!" Mela grinned and held out her hand, and Amelie grabbed it.

"Woohoo!" they yelled and charged toward the ocean, running into the waves so the cold water splashed up their sun-heated bodies and made them scream, and then they let themselves fall and the sea caught them, dancing and bubbling all around them as if it was laughing too.

They dove for shells and pebbles and starfish, had a floppy sword fight with long kelp noodles, and laughed at how short their legs looked in the clear water. The salt tasted delicious, and they licked their fingers until they got too thirsty and tired. They swam as close to the shoreline as they could, letting the warm waves carry them until it was so shallow the sand from the bottom scraped their legs and washed into their swimsuit. Then they jumped up and ran out of the water, kicking up the small waves lapping at the beach and trying to catch the glistening drops in the air.

"Mela?" Mom stood on the beach, shading her eyes with her hand, smiling. "It's time for dinner, sweetheart." Her long blonde hair was fluttering behind her, just like the skirt of her white dress. The top left the shoulders free, and Mela liked how tan and pretty they looked.

"Okay." Mela squatted to pick up her pile of clothes and her Barbie, handing the plastic bath to Amelie.

Amelie always came along when Mom picked up Mela. Her own parents were already inside, watching TV. Mela wished she had a TV. Everyone but Mom had one sitting in the living room, and all the kids in school talked about Knight Rider and Herbie, the Love Bug. Sometimes, Mela tried to pretend she knew what had happened in the latest episode, but she never did. Only when Amelie told her on the way to school.

But if TV was as sad as E.T., it was okay. She had Mom, and Mom either told her stories or read her books. Often, she took Mela into the garden when the air cooled in the evenings and let her help with the beehives. Mela was allowed to puff the smoker, and when Mom opened the hives, it smelled like honey and beeswax. Mom would break off the small extra pieces of comb the bees built on the frames and give them to Mela. The honey dripping from the comb was sweet and sticky, and licking it up was better than watching Knight Rider.

Mela and Amelie stumbled to where Mom waited in her white dress. The sand was dry enough now to squish sideways under their feet, making it hard to walk fast. Mela was tired, and there was still a lot of beach left before the dunes where the plovers lived and the boardwalk started. Mom took their bundles of clothes from them, pinched them under one arm, and held out her hands.

Mela took one, and Amelie took the other.

"I went to the rock pools today," Mom said. "What do you ladies think about having spaghetti with mussels for dinner?"

"Yaaay!" they both screamed as loud as they could.

A gull squawked and rose from the beachgrass, and Mom laughed. "Cool," she said. "We can eat on the stoop and watch the sun go down. Maybe we're extra lucky, and the ice cream truck visits before we walk Amelie home."

Mela knew she'd be super tired after walking her friend home. But she'd rather die than miss out because she loved the slow walk back home to Seasweet Lane when the sky was purple-dark and the flowering beach heather smelled sweet and dry like warm driftwood. Best of all, she would have Mom all to herself.

Amelie looked up at Mom. "Can you carry the bubble bath?"

"Sure." Mom hooked her finger into the window and still managed to hold Amelie's hand. "Did you two have fun?"

"Yeah," Mela said. "Super fun."

"Super fun," Amelie repeated and yawned.

"I can't wait to go sailing." Mom turned and swiveled them around, so they all looked back at the sea. Already, the sinking sun was painting the sky like a page from Mela's Strawberry Shortcake coloring book. Red and pink and golden, the colors dripping all the way into the water and making the waves shimmer.

Whenever she looked at the sea, Mela thought it was the most beautiful she'd ever seen it. But then the next time, she thought it again, and the next time, again. "The sea is always the most beautiful," she said dreamily. "It's perfect every time, just like it is."

Mom pressed her hand for a moment. "Remember that," she said. "You are the same. Always perfect, just like you are."

Mela's stomach growled. "When are you going sailing, Mom?" she asked and looked up.

Mom looked back. "Tomorrow, you little starfish." She smiled. "Amelie's mom is taking you two to have an ice cream in the park and maybe buy new water sandals for Amelie. You can help her pick a color, Mela."

"Yay!" they screamed again, but Mela screamed a little less loudly than before.

Really, she wanted to come sailing. But the boat was too little, Mom had explained, only big enough for two, and obviously Uncle Finn had to go because he was the one who knew how to sail and also he had built the boat by himself and was proud of it.

They would be back by the evening, Mom had said. Maybe earlier, if the weather didn't hold.

Secretly, as they walked on the boardwalk through the warm dunes toward their blue house, Mela hoped the weather wouldn't hold.

She didn't want to go to the park when she could go to the beach. And she didn't want to watch Knight Rider after all.

Mela gripped her mother's hand tighter. "I don't want you to leave," she whispered so Amelie wouldn't hear. "I want you to stay with me."

"I want you to stay too," Amelie said shyly.

"I promise I'll come back," Mom said softly. "I'll always come back because I love you girls."

And then her mother returned Mela's squeeze, and Mela took it as a secret sign that Mom loved her the most.

Chapter 1

The wave crashed into the rugged cliff, spraying upward in a powerful geyser. The killer didn't see it coming; he was standing with his back to the ocean, a black gun pointed at the detective who was middle-aged and lovely and had both a charming accent and a teenage daughter waiting for her at home. Before the killer knew it, the geyser's watery tentacles pulled him, surprised expression and all, into the ocean.

That had happened about fifteen minutes ago. At least it felt like it'd been fifteen minutes.

Ever since, the detective had stood staring at the sky, monologuing aimlessly about the meaning of life.

If she'd jumped into action instead, maybe she could've saved him.

Mela glanced at her husband. Robert's eyes were closed. He wasn't asleep, but he was resting. They'd already had a long week on the campaign trail, and he had to catch the breaks as they came. She elbowed him to indicate the movie was almost over. He'd have to congratulate the director, who was local, then go drink champagne at the mayor's house and predict the movie would become a box office success.

Now the silver-screen sea was shimmering rosy-sweet as if the human sacrifice had calmed it, the waves quieting just so the audience could hear the detective's endless ponderings about... Now it was the rising gas prices. Okay. Still seemed like she should call for backup. Maybe water rescue.

Especially water rescue.

Mela was only the gubernatorial candidate's wife, but they couldn't both close their eyes.

"I'm sorry. Excuse me," Mela whispered and stood, tugging her tight skirt over her knees.

Her husband shook his head without looking. His aide glared at Mela, but he was only in his thirties and couldn't stop her from going to the restroom.

Awkwardly, Mela scooted her way out of the aisle. The theater was closed for the VIP afternoon screening, and once the heavy door swung shut behind her, the corridors with their flecked carpet and windowless walls were empty.

The tiny bathroom stalls smelled of stale popcorn and recycled air.

Suddenly, Mela gagged. Her forehead broke into a sweat, and dots started to dance in her peripheral vision.

She backed out of the stall and went to the sink to cool her wrists. The rushing of water into the bowl sounded like... It sounded like... With a trembling hand, she screwed the faucet closed, but her knees softened as if the water had gotten into her joints. Mela leaned against the tiled wall and slowly lowered herself until she was sitting on the floor. She tilted her head back, focusing on taking slow, deep breaths that she held captive for as long as she could.

They'd stopped at a seafood restaurant for lunch and a photo opportunity, and Mela had had mussels in wine sauce. One of them must've been bad.

When the ringing in her ears turned to a hum and the dizziness cleared, she stood and propped open the tiny window, closing her eyes and drinking in the mall's parking lot air. It smelled of tar and hot cars.

Mela pulled a paper towel from the dispenser and blotted her face. A last tug on the stupid skirt—Armani, too tight, never again—a last deep breath, and she was ready to dive back in.

The movie should be over soon. Mela squared her shoulders, fixed a smile on her face, and pushed open the door, high-heeling her way back through the eerie corridors to the theater. She slipped back into the dark.

Her smile dropped. The screen was gray, shimmering only with a faint fluorescent afterglow. The theater seats were empty.

"What?" Mela whispered, walking down to the aisle they'd all occupied only minutes ago.

But nobody was sitting there anymore.

Rob was gone. The aides were gone, the assistant was gone, the mayor, select community college students, and local director were gone. Mela turned. Even the window of the projector room was dark.

She went into the aisle.

Her clam shell clutch still sat on the arm of her seat. Mela snatched it up. Had people just left her purse? Her *phone* was in there. Rob's entire calendar was on it. It was a total safety hazard to leave it where anyone could grab it.

Mela turned, hurrying as fast as her heels allowed back out into the corridor. It was as eerily quiet as before, and when she got to the front entrance, the popcorn machine stood abandoned, the ticket counter was deserted, the space between one and the other empty.

In disbelief, Mela went to the glass door and pushed.

It didn't budge.

She peered outside. Rob's campaign bus was gone.

They had forgotten her.

Chapter 2

A wave of shame washed over Mela as she stared at the empty parking lot.

Had she become so forgettable that her husband didn't even notice whether she was by his side? How could he have missed her absence when the movie was over? Had he overlooked the purse sitting abandoned on her seat?

She sent a text and then called Rob, but his phone was on silent and the call immediately went to voice mail.

Same for Johanna, Mela's personal assistant.

Mela let her phone sink. The only other thing she could think of was to text someone else in their group and ask if they could come and break her out of the movie theater. It wasn't a great idea because PR claimed someone in Rob's team leaked information to the press. Social media would have a field day with a story this embarrassing.

It was better to wait. As soon as he'd notice she was missing, Robert would look at his phone and see her text, and then he'd send Johanna to pick up Mela.

Mela didn't know where she should wait to be picked up and how to behave when her assistant finally got there. Pretend she was so busy on her phone she'd barely noticed they'd left her behind? Be mad, fire Johanna for ignoring Mela's call? Be quiet, let it pass? Laugh, say she fainted in the bathroom because her skirt's waistband was too tight?

All of it was embarrassing. Especially since the entire bus campaign had been Mela's idea; she'd been the one setting it up. She'd hired the team. She'd called the mayor and the local director and made sure there'd be duck breast canapés and champagne so Rob could look good and get elected.

Mela sent another text, and then she started to wander because if someone saw her standing by the glass like an abandoned puppy, she'd die of humiliation. They would know who she was.

Or would they?

Mela had always thought of herself as one of the drivers of her husband's career. Rob's policies were sound. They were important. Mela knew Rob was going to make the ethically and morally sound decisions the state needed.

The opposition also had some solid strategies, but Rob's had an edge, and his election was where all of Mela's energy went. Had gone in the past as well, since she'd been working for the cause since they'd married. And they'd married young. Twenty-eight years ago, this September.

She stopped, staring at a movie poster. Deep down in the green sea, a humanoid amphibian—amphibian humanoid?—was hugging a woman. It was a weird picture, and Mela turned away quickly.

It had been half an hour since she'd found the theater empty, and who knew how long since everyone had left. Maybe when she'd stood to go to the bathroom, the movie had already been ending. And Rob hadn't missed her once all this time.

Mela found a chair behind the ticket counter and sat. She could try texting other people, tell them that she'd been forgotten in a movie theater and if they could please come get her. She could call the police, go on record, and give the opposition fodder. *Gubernatorial candidate Robert Beckett can't keep track of his wife—how will he keep track of unemployment rates?*

Rob would be hopping mad.

Or Mela could call an Uber and hope the driver wouldn't recognize her.

Yes. That was the best, as long as she could get out of the building without setting off the fire alarm. Rob didn't need that sort of publicity.

Mela started to walk around the small theater until she found an unmarked door that didn't have a fire exit sign. Holding her breath, she pushed.

The door opened. Almost in disbelief, Mela stepped out into the sun.

It had been that easy.

Click your heels and go home.

Compared to the dim inside, the outside was bright and hot. The air in the parking lot still smelled of asphalt and warm metal, but after the stale, buttery air in the theater, even that was a relief.

Mela called herself an Uber.

Ten minutes later, she climbed into a red Ford Focus that had seen better days. The driver was a young woman with long, blond hair, who smiled into the rearview mirror. "Hi."

"Hi." Mela buckled in.

"The address you want to go to—is that the mayor's house?" The young woman flicked the blinker and pulled away from the curb.

"Yes," Mela said. "It is."

"I think they have some event going on there," the young woman said. "I drove by earlier, and a bunch of cars had parked on the street."

"Oh really?"

"Yes." The young woman glanced at her again. "I'm sure it'll be a mess."

Mela turned to the window. "Hopefully, things will work out," she said. But pushing the right political measures was sometimes a messy process. For a brief moment, she considered engaging the woman in a political conversation to see where she stood. But she wanted a break to recover her composure and plan her entrance, and she wanted to get to the event before anyone started missing her. Slipping in unnoticed would be best.

"My mom used to work for a rich guy. Richer than the mayor." The Focus stopped at a traffic light, and the driver rolled down her window. "His parties made such a mess; you should hear the stories the cleaning ladies told Mom." Again the driver smiled at Mela in the mirror. "Do you have any good stories?"

Mela realized her driver quite literally expected a mess. Litter on the floor, crumbs, that sort of thing.

She smiled back. "Good stories? About what now?"

"About parties or something."

"Oh." Mela sank back into the seat. Her driver hadn't recognized Mela at all. "No, I'm afraid not."

They drove on in silence. It was slow because of the traffic. Mela's glanced at the driver's tan shoulders and honey-blond hair. The sun coming through the open window made it shine, and the wind made it flutter.

It was the prettiest sight Mela had seen for a long while.

She leaned forward. "Excuse me, how far is it?"

"Like another ten minutes. We're going past the highway in a moment, and most of these cars will get on. No worries."

"Do you mind if I change the destination?"

The tan shoulders shrugged. "I've nothing planned. I don't mind driving around all night, as long as you don't mind paying."

"Could you pull over at the gas station here, please?"

"Okay."

"Gas is on me if you need to fill up."

The blonde turned around, eyes narrowed. "That's never happened before."

"It's happening now."

"Is this a test? Are you going to mess with my ratings if I say yes?"

"Your ratings? Oh. Your Uber ratings. No, of course not. Consider it a tip. I'll never tell a soul." She dug a fifty from her purse and handed it to the woman. "What's your name?"

"Linda." The woman took the fifty.

"I'd like to go to Bay Harbor," Mela said. "Do you think you can drive me?"

"Bay Harbor? Isn't that near Sandville? That's like two or three hours." Linda tilted her head. "I wasn't... I mean, I guess I could." She waved the fifty. "Yeah, all right. I can get you to Bay Harbor."

Mela took a quick, excited breath.

She'd started something just now.

For the first time in years, she had no plan. There was nothing on her mind but sun and wind and wanting to be in a beautiful place that she loved.

"Would you mind if I go get a snack?" She pointed at the station. This close to the highway, the store was big enough to carry souvenirs and local swag.

"Feel free." Linda gestured at the building. "I already got paid, in case you plan on running off on me."

"I'll be back," Mela promised. "Don't leave without me."

Linda nodded.

Mela got out of the Focus and hurried into the gas station; she didn't want to lose her ride, but she couldn't stand the designer skirt riding up one more moment.

The store had a rack of blue T-shirts. One kind said *Gas till I Pass* in yellow letters, the other *Beach Babe*. Mela grabbed the beach babe one, a dusty pack of comfort leggings, a pair of sunglasses, a pink baseball cap, and the last pair of pink flip-flops.

"Goodness." Linda had parked by the store and come inside.

"I'd like to change really quick." Mela tugged her skirt back in place. "The heels are killing me."

"Sure, go ahead."

"Would you be able to buy us some water and snacks and...I don't know, just a couple of sandwiches and coffees for the trip?" Mela pulled another fifty-dollar bill from her clutch.

Linda raised her eyebrows to indicate anything was good for her and held out her hand. "Are you in trouble?" she asked. "Can I do anything to help?"

"I'm fine." Mela pressed the money into the young woman's palm. "I'm just a little fed up with my job."

Linda grinned. "You do you. Go change. I'll get supplies."

Mela made a beeline for the bathrooms. It wasn't a stall but a good-sized room that doubled as storage for boxes of toilet paper and kitchen towels, and she changed as quickly as she could from the expensive suit into her new outfit. Finally, she could breathe, and everything fit loosely instead of pinching. She stuffed her suit in the bag, took the high heels into her hand, and flip-flopped out of the room.

When Linda saw her, she gave Mela a thumbs up. "You look all right," she said. "Cool, cool. I got us coke and peanuts and paid for your stuff too, so we're all set."

Mela had pictured something more like apples and water, but coke and peanuts worked as well. They stowed their purchases in the back seat of the Focus, and Mela got into the passenger seat.

"It's three now," Linda muttered, adjusting her rearview mirror. "And it's a two-hour drive, isn't it?" She tapped on her phone for a map.

"Yes," Mela said and buckled in. "Two hours and fourteen minutes."

"Spot on." Linda pushed her phone into a plastic claw holder so she could see the map while driving. "Did you look it up?" She started the car and backed out of the parking spot.

"I did yesterday night when I got here," Mela said. "I always look it up."

For a while, Linda drove quietly. When they were on the highway, she stirred. "Are your folks in Bay Harbor?"

"My mother used to live there." Mela watched the trees zip past. "But the house has stood empty for decades."

Linda glanced over her shoulder and accelerated into the right lane. "Are you back all the time? I would if I had a house in Bay Harbor. I can't even afford a hotel, let alone one near the sea."

Mela smiled. Bay Harbor was too small for expensive hotels to take notice of the town. "There used to be a small motel when I was little, but I don't know if it's there anymore."

"I love a sunny beach," Linda said dreamily. "If it doesn't work out with my boyfriend, maybe I'll try and get a job near the coast."

"There used to be jobs at Bay Port University, though that's thirty miles south of Bay Harbor," Mela said. "My mom worked there on and off as a lab assistant."

"Yeah? I might look into it. I have a degree in social work," Linda said. "Maybe I should use it for a change."

"Are you living together with your boyfriend?" Mela asked, and for the next hour or so, Linda talked about herself. Mela listened and commiserated, but now and then, she zoned out and followed her own thoughts.

Rob still hadn't called. Nobody else had, either.

Was it possible they still hadn't missed her? Mela knew the calendar by heart. After the champagne reception came a big dinner, hosted a town over. They'd be on the way now, her seat on the bus empty. How could Rob overlook her absence?

Or maybe the better question was when had he last noticed her presence?

"I told him that's why I should go back home," Linda said, her voice wavering. "You know?"

"Yes," Mela said, pulling herself back to the moment. "Yes, I do know. I hope you will, my dear. I'm sure they'd be happy to see you again."

Linda swallowed a couple of times, and then she popped a green piece of chewing gum from a blister and into her mouth. The smell of peppermint filled the car. "Now you. What's going on with you?"

"Very little," Mela said, feeling the truth of it. "Very little is going on with me. I just want to stop by my mother's house to take a breather."

"You have kids?"

Mela nodded. "Three beautiful kids, all of them adults, all of them out of the house. They've got their own lives."

"Are they happy?"

"I think they are." She smiled, thinking of them.

"Sounds like you've got it all figured out," Linda said, and then they both fell quiet.

At some point, an accident slowed them down. As they stood in the line that jammed the highway, a honeybee landed on the windshield.

"Nope." Linda shook her head. "I hate wasps. I'm allergic." She reached to flick on the wipers and smush the bee, but Mela held out a hand to stop her.

"It's not a wasp. It's a honeybee," she said gently. "She's just catching her breath. Let her live; she'll take off again in a second."

"She? Why she?"

"They're all girls. All the bees in a hive are sisters."

Leaning forward, Mela studied the bee. Her mother, Julie, had dreamed of having a proper beeyard and selling honey at the local farmers markets.

"What about the boys?" Linda squinted at the honeybee too.

"Drones only stick around a few days. They don't gather honey, so the girls don't allow them to stay in the hive."

"Smart." Linda nodded her appreciation.

The bee took off again, ready to resume her search for nectar. Or maybe, Mela thought, she was ready to return home to her family.

She checked her cell phone. Only another hour to Bay Harbor.

They were almost there.

CHAPTER 3

"That's your house?" Linda peered through the windshield.

It was almost seven. There'd been the traffic knot and a restroom stop, and once Linda had to pull over to talk with her boyfriend on the phone.

"That's it," Mela said. She pulled out her wallet. "What do I owe you?"

Linda tapped at her Uber app and then showed the screen to Mela. Mela paid, adding a generous tip.

"Are you sure?" Linda looked at the banknotes in her hand. "That's a lot, even for a two-hour drive."

"Yes," Mela said. "Thank you, Linda. For the drive and the good company."

"Well, thank *you*." Linda rolled the money into the cup holder. "Are you going to be okay? I'm getting mixed vibes from this place," she said, her lips going on to quietly add, *and you*.

Mela nodded. Her hand was already on the handle. She wanted to get out and put her feet on the sun-warmed ground, feel that it was real and that she had arrived. "Yes," she assured her young driver.

"Everything is going to be okay. Work has been busy, but I'm taking a little time for myself now."

"A seaside vacation sounds like the right medicine." Linda leaned back. She still looked unconvinced, as if seeing Mela's house made her second guess staying was a good idea.

Bay Harbor meant so much more than an old house.

Smiling, Mela opened the door and got out. The air smelled of salt, and behind the house, she could hear the gentle rushing of waves. For ten years, the sound had been her childhood lullaby. She leaned back to look into the car. "Thank you so much for driving me, Linda. Let me just grab my bags before you leave."

"Make sure to take what's left of the snacks," Linda replied. "It doesn't hurt to have some food on you since you don't have a car and can't just nip over to the nearest supermarket."

Mela nodded. A small mom-and-pop market used to be only a short walk away, but who knew if it still was where she remembered it.

Linda rolled her window down. "Are you sure you want to stay here? I'm happy to drive you to Sandville. I know they have restaurants and hotels and all that. Or, listen, you can come back with me. No charge."

"I'm all right. Don't worry, Linda." Mela had been dreaming of coming back ever since she'd been forced to leave. "I'm glad I'm finally here. Thanks again. If you ever decide to take a break yourself, look me up, okay?" She pulled out her bags and closed the doors.

"I might do that. Bye then." Linda waved and pulled back into the empty street. Then she drove away, the engine sound slowly fading until it was quiet. Only a thrush was singing, hidden in the lush foliage of a lilac bush.

Mela stood, looking at the house.

She'd come back only once, and then only for an afternoon. A week after she'd turned eighteen, a yellow manilla folder addressed to her had appeared in the mailbox. It'd been from the law firm in charge of Julie's estate. Inside had been a key, a deed, and a brief note explaining the house and property were now Mela's to do with as she liked.

Soon after, her adoptive parents, Angela and Harry, had taken her to Bay Harbor. Mela had gotten into Harvard, and the family had made a detour before dropping her off at college.

They'd only stayed an hour.

Angela had been teary the entire trip, struggling with the fact that the last of her adopted children was flying the nest. Harry had been grumpy over the detour taking them in the opposite direction on an already long drive, and both parents worried Mela would miss the freshman orientation meeting.

Mela had barely had time to match her lovely, warm childhood memories to the empty shell of the small blue house she was visiting. She only knew its spirit, though not yet its walls, had cracked and crumbled. It had felt different from what she remembered.

This time, it was worse. She realized Linda had offered to take her back because now, the walls were cracking as well.

The salt winds of the Atlantic had hugged the little house too long and too hard. The wooden boards of the siding didn't quite seem to fit together anymore, and the faded paint bubbled and peeled. The roof was blotchy and missed shingles. The glass of the kitchen window looking out on the street was broken.

Behind the broken window, Julie's lace curtain, once white and now yellowed, moved as if a ghostly hand was brushing it aside. But the evening breeze was also brushing Mela's hair from her forehead, and she knew only too well that nobody was waiting for her inside.

Last time, they'd hurried inside, practically running through the rooms before sitting in the kitchen for an awkward meal of fast food sandwiches before whisking away again.

This time, Mela meant to give herself time to feel that this had once been her home and that she belonged. She scanned the front of the house, giving her mind and body time to adjust after the long, fast drive. She had arrived and was standing on her two feet.

Julie's grandparents had bought the place way back when oceanfront property in Maine cost a song and a dance. To the right, the lot bordered a neighbor hidden behind a hedge of lilac bushes. To the left sprawled the remnants of an old apple orchard. The trees still bore fruits, and Mela spotted bright-red apples hanging from the branches, looking more appetizing than any wrapped snacks ever would. Julie had made apple pies and apple sauce, but she'd most loved the trees' tiny white flowers. They nurtured honeybees in the spring, when the overwintered, hungry colonies needed nectar the most.

Clutching her plastic bags, Mela walked up the path that led from the gate to the house.

Julie had planted flowers and bushes so that unless snow covered the ground, something sweet always bloomed. Even now, though the house itself looked to be in poor shape, the front yard was exploding with cheerful flowers.

Standing by the door, Mela spotted white pillows of rockcress and pastel columbines, purple bee balm and black-eyed Susans, clouds of fluffy fleabane, and the delicate pink tones of false dragonhead.

The floral scents mixed with the salty air, attracting visiting honeybees, fuzzy bumblebees, and tiny solitary bees that shimmered metallic blues and greens and were no bigger than a grain of wheat. Magnificent tiger swallowtails weaved in and out among the bees, dipping peacefully from flower to flower to sip nectar.

Mela took a moment to savor the fragrant air and watch the small foragers. When she felt more grounded, she tried the door handle. It was locked.

Of course it was locked. The key was in the same envelope it had arrived in, filed away in a metal cabinet in Mela's home office.

Hoping she remembered right, Mela went around the house and with a stick parted the thick ragweed growing at the base of the tree nearest to the house. She experienced a moment of growing unease when she couldn't find what she was looking for. But finally, closer to the trunk than she remembered, Mela spotted the three stones the sea had polished into marbled eggs.

Relieved, Mela pulled out a few handfuls of weeds before she prodded the rocks from the soil, uncovering the hollow below. In it was a small glass jar and in that, a key.

Mela wiggled out the jar, dusted it off, and held it up so she could inspect the key.

Julie had been the last person to touch it. Mela had watched her bury the jar so Mela could always get back in the house.

Mela had to use the hem of her beach babe T-shirt to unscrew the rusted lid, but she managed to get it off and shake out the key. Her heart was beating a little harder as the cool metal hit her palm, knocking against her ribs in anticipation.

The key fit the lock, and after a few wiggles and pushes, the front door creaked open. Mela took a breath as if she was about to dive into deep water, and then she stepped inside.

Suddenly, she was home. It had taken her nearly forty years, but her heart still remembered the feeling.

She stood, trying to take it in. This was the place where she'd been so happy the first ten years of her life. Then, her childhood had ended with a night of absolute terror.

Mela blew out the breath that had carried her over the threshold. She'd had therapy. Lots of it.

Grief came in waves, like the sea. And like the tide, it ebbed again.

She closed the door on the sinking sun. It was as pleasantly warm inside as outside.

Slowly, Mela walked on. Into the living room with the old couch she and her mom had cuddled on and into the big cheery kitchen with its fern-green cabinets. The eggshell fridge smelled musty inside but was clean and empty, the plug lying on the floor next to the outlet.

In the bathroom, the ceiling paint had peeled off and scattered onto the floor. Everywhere, dust motes floated through the last rays of sunlight like lost souls. Mela tried to open a window, but the frame was warped, and she had to push a couple of times before the clean, clear evening air came streaming in.

Upstairs were four bedrooms. Mom's, Mela's with her tiny bed and play rug, and two unused ones. Mela peeked at the boxes in one of the closets. Julie had always meant to check the contents and store them in the attic but never spared time to do it.

Everything inside looked scruffier than Mela remembered, and a lot dustier.

But the sea outside the windows was bright and beautiful, waving like a long-lost friend, and she could see that the old garden surrounding the patio had as many flowers and blooms as the front yard.

Mela wanted to explore it all. She wanted to walk down to the beach, put her feet in the water, and let the small, white-crested waves wash up her legs.

Instead, she went back into the living room where she'd left her purse and pulled out her phone. There was a text from Rob, sent a minute ago.

Where are you?

Mela stared at it.

That was it? That was the sum total of his concern after leaving the theater without her, going to the mayor's reception, and the dinner? Where did he think she was?

She cleared her throat. Well, she was in Bay Harbor. He couldn't possibly know that. And she was perfectly fine.

After almost thirty years of marriage, she knew to stay calm when her feelings were hurt. Rob was pragmatic. He wouldn't understand her upset. Mela considered sending a text back, but after a short internal struggle, she gave in and called.

The call went straight to her husband's answering machine.

Something inside Mela ripped. A string connecting them that had been strung too taut. A contract they'd signed on paper turned brittle.

"Hello, Rob," she said. "You left while I was in the bathroom in the movie theater, feeling unwell. I went to Mom's house in Bay Harbor to take care of a few things. I'm all right, and I'll see you soon. Bye."

She ended the call and sat on the sofa. Even though her voice had been cool, her cheeks felt flushed.

She'd never ever left Rob hanging before. No matter how busy he was, his campaign had always been their campaign. She'd faithfully supported him because he was her husband and because politics mattered. It was a way to help people. It was a way to make the world a better place.

But the family had spent the last decade in the public's eye and Mela knew her marriage had paid a price. Winning the race had seemed more important, though. The good of many over her and Rob's happiness.

She had to pee and checked the bathroom, but the toilet bowls were dry. There was also no water for washing off the day.

Mela opened Linda's snack bag and peered inside. One more soda to get her through the night, a single-serve bag of trail mix, a chocolate bar, and the apples outside.

Her phone was down to the last bar. Hoping it wouldn't die, she googled for the motel that used to be in Bay Harbor. If it was still there, it would have electricity and a bathroom. To her delight, Mela found a place listed that matched and tapped the phone link.

"Seaside Motel," a man answered. "Hello?"

"Hi. Do you have a room available tonight?" Mela asked. "And a way to get me there? I'm at the blue house on Seasweet Lane."

"The blue house?"

“Well, it used to be blue. Now it’s sun bleached. It’s house number 12.”

“That house is abandoned,” the man said.

“No, it’s not. I just didn’t have time to come until now. Do you have a room?”

“I sure do.” The man sighed.

“And could you pick me up? I don’t have a car.”

“Sure. Hang on tight. I’ll be there in five.”

“Thanks.” With a tinkle, Mela’s phone shut down because it was out of battery. She tucked it into her purse and gathered her bags.

There was so much to do. So much to look at and so much to feel, so much to fix, and so much to... So much to...

Mela covered her face with her hand. But unlike in the movie theater, it wasn’t panic that made her feel like she was floating.

It was giddy joy at finally being in Bay Harbor bubbling up from the cracks inside her.

She dropped her hands, feeling a huge smile spread over her face. This night, she’d make a list. Buy supplies and call utilities.

She could stay one week. Seven days to reconnect with her past, to swim in the sea, and to sit on the patio that called through the glass of the living room sliding doors.

Mela went outside and sat on the front step where, warmed by the evening sun, caressed by the sea breeze, and surrounded by fragrant blossoms, she waited for her ride.

CHAPTER 4

The sky was turning into burnished gold by the time Mela heard the sound of an engine.

She stood and went to the fence to look. A motorbike was speeding toward her. It was moss green and had a one-wheeled sidecar buzzing along.

"Oh heck no," Mela whispered. "Tell me he's coming for someone else."

Riding the bike was a silver-helmeted man in jeans and a white button-down shirt the wind hugged against his stomach. He pulled into the same spot Linda had left earlier, braced a long leg on the ground, and pulled off the helmet. His hair was wild, his eyes blue, and his smile kind.

"Hi," he said.

"Hello." Mela gripped her plastic bags harder. "Are you here for me?"

He looked at the house. "If this is the formerly blue house on Seasweet, then yes. I'm here for you." He nodded at the egg-shaped sidecar.

"I'm forty-seven," Mela said in her let's-be-reasonable voice usually reserved for overheating town hall meetings. "I'm five feet five inches tall and weigh one hundred and forty-five pounds. I'm not sure I should get into that."

"It's very comfortable," the man promised. "By the way, I'm Peter." His eyes narrowed slightly as he looked at her.

Mela tilted her head, wondering what she'd missed. "I'm Pamela," she said.

"Pamela," he repeated slowly. "Pamela."

It wasn't exactly an unusual name. Maybe he was fishing for her last name? "Beckett," she added, feeling it would mean nothing to him. This was Maine, and the team rarely ran their out-of-state TV ads where the camera swept past her and the kids on its way to Rob. Nobody would recognize her based on the short exposure.

"Pam Beckett?"

"Mela, actually." She returned her focus to the bike.

Peter patted down his helmet hair. "Well, Mela Beckett, this is it," he said encouragingly. "This is your ride. Would you like to try even though you're forty-seven? The alternative is walking."

Something in his words made her grin. There was cheekiness simmering below the polite ultimatum. "And how old are you?" she asked back. There was more silver in his dark hair than her own.

"Old enough to drive you," he said and grinned back. "Hop on in, it's getting dark, and I'm not leaving you stranded here. It's too far to walk in flip-flops."

Mela swallowed a sigh. "I'll try everything once." Luckily, she wasn't wearing the tight Armani suit anymore. She'd never get her leg high enough to climb in.

Peter held out a hand to help her hop in, as he'd called it, and Mela took it. To her surprise, she needed no awkward gymnastics to enter the egg because of a step and a considerate cutout in the side. She settled into the seat. It was wobbly but doable.

"It's okay," she said, unable to keep the surprise from her voice.

If Rob could see her now—but she wasn't going to think about him. She was going to go to the motel and look out at the sea and take a break. It was fine. She was fine.

The bike wobbled again when Peter mounted the machine. "Here." He handed her his silver helmet. "You should wear this."

Mela stared at it. "I'm *forty*-seven. Not seven."

He chuckled. "Do the forty extra years make your noodle any less precious?"

"My what?"

He raised an eyebrow. "Your head. Your noodle."

"Noodle?"

"Yes."

"Fine." She took the helmet. The last time she had shared a hat was...maybe half a decade ago when her daughter Kimmie had still been at home and they'd shared a collection of winter hats.

Without waiting for her to put it on, Peter revved the engine. The sidecar swayed, and then it scooted forward like a fat bumblebee out to attack. The bike jerked into the driveway and back out onto the street, turning around.

"Hey!" Mela dropped the helmet into her lap and grabbed the bar in front of her. "Easy!"

She was pretty sure Peter couldn't hear. He accelerated, going faster and faster.

With one hand, Mela stowed her plastic bags between her feet to keep them from flying away. With the other, she pushed her gas station glasses on her nose. Then she smacked the helmet onto her head, fastened the strap, and held on tight.

Once she let go of trying to control the vehicle, the ride became fun. Mela leaned when Peter leaned and straightened when the bike straightened.

"It's like a fair ride!" she yelled.

"What?" he yelled back.

"A fair ride? A ride at the fair?"

He raised a mystified eyebrow, raked his hair out of his eyes, and pointed. "Almost there."

"Keep your hands on the steering... The thing, the bar!" Mela yelled. "Please!"

They were flying past flowering hydrangeas, faded wood houses, small shops, and the green spaces tucked in between. Mela remembered walking these streets, the scents of sea and summer in the air, visiting the shops and homes of school friends. Memories floated up like soap bubbles; one after the other, bursting before she'd seen her fill.

"It's so pretty," she whispered to herself, the wind whisking the words from her lips.

In a distracted moment, Rob had once said Bay Harbor was just another small town.

It was true, too. But it was her small town.

Peter slowed and turned onto Main, and a few moments later, he pulled into the motel court. The white shell fragments filling the court crunched under the tires as the engine puttered to a stop.

Mela sat in her egg close to the ground, ears ringing from the whistling of the wind.

Peter put a foot on the ground for balance and looked down to where she was. "Here we are."

Mela pried her fingers from the bar. "It's different from what I remember," she said.

"Yes." Peter held out his hand, and Mela loosened the strap under her chin and handed him her helmet. *His* helmet. His helmet.

"I'm afraid I was away too long," he said. "The damage was done by the time I came back. But I plan on fixing it."

Mela unfolded herself. Her left knee was a little bruised because she'd banged it on the side of the egg going into a curve.

"You were away?" she asked. "Me too. I grew up here. Well, until I was ten, anyway."

"I lived in Africa for a while," Peter said. "I was doing research in the Serengeti. But then Dad got sick, and well...it took me too long to understand how much trouble the motel was in. I did what I could, but you don't become a biologist to get rich. Nor are there so many guests staying here."

"I'm sorry," Mela said. All the hotels and budget inns were in Sandville and Bay Port, and each city had miles of beach to keep paying guests in town. "I know it's a drop on a hot stone, but I will stay here."

"All right, all right, all right." Peter got off the bike and waved her to follow him. "Let's get you checked in." He started toward the building. "I'll find a way to spruce her up again. The old girl just needs to get her groove back."

"Her and me both," Mela muttered, unfolding herself from the sidecar. "At least the hydrangeas are still lovely!" she called after Peter. "Hey, wait for me. I don't know where to go."

"There's only one way!" he called back over his shoulder and disappeared through a lavender door.

Mela clipped her sunglasses to the neck of her T-shirt, slapped her ball cap on her head, and fished her plastic bags out of the foot space.

The motel was an L-shaped two-story building with an iron rail running along the upper level and a staircase at the bend. The roof was flat, and the walls a faded pink, which made the building look like a '50s Friday night hop that served teenagers banana split ice cream sundaes.

Mela remembered bright colors, a pretty scalloped edge hiding the gutter, and curtains behind the windows.

There were no curtains or gutter linings anymore. But there was climbing hydrangea and wisteria, potted bougainvilleas and trumpet flowers, and the lush plants made up for much of the missing curtains and fading paint. Mela wished she'd kept quiet earlier. On second glance, it was clear that a lot of love went into maintaining the place, even if it needed more work, and she hoped she'd not hurt her host's feelings.

The lavender door opened again. "It's in here," Peter said, looking out. "This is the reception."

"Yes, I'm coming," Mela said, and suddenly she remembered him. Maybe it was the way he stood at the door, waiting for her.

"You're *Peter*," she said. "Peter Townson."

He smiled. "About time, little Mela," he said. "I thought you'd become too famous to remember me."

"Oh goodness!" She went to where he stood and took both his hands into hers. Peter was the older brother of a childhood friend of hers, and their ways had crossed now and then in the small town. She remembered her friend's infectious laughter and his sky-blue eyes. Peter's eyes were the same; she should have known right away he was Charlie's brother. "Where's Charlie?" she asked eagerly.

Peter's face darkened. "He's left us."

She pulled back. "Oh. Oh no. I'm so sorry." Charlie had been in her class; they were the same age.

"Oh. I mean, he's moved away. He's fine. He's fine. I think."

"So he's still...?"

"Alive. Yes. He's very much alive. I think."

"Oh." She exhaled with relief. "I'm so glad. Charlie was my friend in school. I liked him very much." She stepped past Peter into the room. The light was dim compared to outside, and it smelled of lemons and linoleum flooring.

"Yes, you did." Peter sounded wry. He switched on the light and went behind the registration counter, tapping on the computer keyboard. The screen stayed dark. He pressed the power button.

"Did I make a fool of myself?" Mela asked, setting her plastic bags down. "It's so long ago, I can barely remember."

"No more than the rest of us," Peter said distractedly. "Um, one night?" He smacked the computer screen and then gave up and opened an old-fashioned ledger on the counter.

"Yes, please." Mela picked up a pencil stub—the only writing utensil available—and signed where he pointed. "Are there mosquitoes in the rooms?"

"No," he said. "But maybe there are starfish."

She looked up, startled, meeting his eyes. "What do you mean, starfish?"

"Just kidding. Don't worry. They try to stay in the sea."

A strange change of mood had come over her driver. Why, Mela didn't know. Maybe it was the state of the motel. Maybe because she'd taken a while to recognize him. But it'd been so long ago...

She opened her purse and pulled out her phone, automatically swiping for her schedule before registering the black screen.

Right. Her battery was drained.

She tucked her phone back, suddenly realizing she'd criticized the motel twice now. First, by pointing out it wasn't in the best shape, and then by suggesting she expected bugs. It had been a routine question because Robert hated bugs, but Peter didn't know that.

He turned the ledger toward him, adding the date behind her signature.

She laid her hand on the open page. "Wait," she said. "Could you make it a week?"

He stopped writing. "I can," he said. "An entire week, are you sure? Starfish and all?"

Mela smiled. She couldn't recall the last time anyone had mentioned starfish this often. "Yes, I'm sure."

"Okay then," Peter said. He used the pencil's eraser to rub out the line, and then he added a new date.

"Seven days," Mela said happily.

Peter laid his hand on hers and patted it once. "Welcome back, Pamela Beckett," he said. "I hope you'll enjoy your stay."

"Thanks," she said. "I'm sure I will."

He turned to a board on the wall behind, picked an old-fashioned key, and handed it to her. "Room twenty it is."

"Okay. Upstairs, downstairs?" She gathered her plastic bags.

"Upstairs, turn right, all the way at the end."

She looked at the key. “Why all the way at the end?” Her pain from being forgotten stirred again. Why should she be so far away?

Peter closed the ledger and leaned on the counter. “Because the room all the way at the end has the best view of the sea. You love the sea, Mela. Do you remember?”

Almost, she flushed with embarrassment at assuming she wasn’t wanted.

Here, she belonged.

“I remember,” she said quietly. “Thank you.”

“You’re welcome.” The corners of Peter’s eyes crinkled. “I’ll see you tomorrow morning.”

Chapter 5

Mela climbed the staircase and walked along the balcony, all the way to the end. As promised, number twenty was the last door. The key turned easily, and Mela went inside and felt for the light switch.

As a child, it had never occurred to her that she might be staying here one day. It was exciting.

The light flicked on. The room was small and simple. A narrow wooden desk with a chair, a midsize TV on a dresser, a cleanly made bed, and a nightstand with a reading lamp. Beside the door was a bathroom with a sink, toilet, and shower, and on the other side was a shallow closet built into the wall. It wasn't fancy, but it was clean and dry and perfectly fine for a few days.

Mela set her bags on the desk. Over the bed hung a photograph of a family of cheetahs. "No starfish after all," she whispered. Maybe she'd get a picture postcard with one and put it on the nightstand.

She took off her baseball cap and pulled the bobby pins from her hair, shaking out her braided French bun. She had a lot of hair, and up-dos hurt her scalp by the end of the day. She brought the pins in the bathroom and washed her face and hands. The mirror showed no new silver in the hazel strands, just a few old ones. She'd stubbornly decided against dying or plucking them, even though the PR team was regularly asking her to do it.

Massaging her neck with one hand, Mela went to open the sliding door to the balcony and stepped out. There was enough space for a chair. A faded-pink cement wall reaching halfway to the banister separated her balcony from the next.

The sea was almost the same velvety plum color as the sky, darkest on the horizon where the two met and lighter where it turned into amethyst waves dancing onto the beach and disappearing like ghosts in the sand.

"See?" asked a voice below her. "It's pretty."

When she looked down, she saw Peter in the narrow backyard, smoking a slim cigarillo. Its fragrance mixed with that of roses and night-blooming jasmine just unfolding its starry flowers.

"It's a beautiful view."

He held the cigarillo up, smiling an apology. "My only vice. I get one in the evening if I score a six or higher for the day."

"Score in what?" Mela smiled back.

He took a moment to consider. "General behavior."

"So you did pretty well today?"

"It's been all right." He nodded.

"Who are you talking to, Peter?" A light came on in the balcony beside Mela. She leaned around the privacy wall.

An elderly lady was sitting in her open balcony door, her chair's legs half inside, half out. She was wearing a nightgown and robe. Her hands were lying flat on her knees as if she were meditating.

"Hi," Mela said and waved a greeting. She hadn't realized she had a neighbor who was enjoying the evening quiet. "I'm Mela. I'll be staying here for a week."

There was a gardenia in her neighbor's window, and the bed had a knitted afghan on it. Maybe that was a doily on the TV. Or maybe the lady was using the TV to dry her clothes. Mela couldn't tell.

"Hi, hon." The old lady waved back. "Where are you from? New Jersey? New York?"

"I'm a little bit from here," Mela said. "I grew up in Bay Harbor, though I've lived in New Hampshire for almost thirty years."

"Do you have a nice house in New Hampshire?"

"A very nice house." Modern, three fridges, two dishwashers, too many rooms, but the kids still came home for Christmas and Easter.

The lady leaned forward. "Are you alone, or is someone else over there with you?"

"It's just me."

"What are you doing here all by yourself? Are you married?"

"Yes, I'm married."

"So?"

"Uh." Mela pushed her hair back. "I'm looking after my mother's house."

"Which house is that?"

"It's the blue house on Seasweet," Mela said. That's how Mom used to tell people where they lived. Maybe in the decades since, more people had painted their houses blue.

The lady stirred, pulling her robe closer around herself. Mela couldn't see her face. There was no moon out yet, and her neighbor's room was lit behind her.

"The blue house on Seasweet," the lady repeated softly.

"Do you know it?"

"That used to belong to the bee lady," came the reply. "Julie Palmer lived there."

Mela's heart picked up speed. Someone remembered Julie? But of course they did—they even remembered Mela. Peter did, anyway, and Mela had only been a little girl.

Julie had been an adult, a young, single mother with long hair and floaty dresses.

Of course people remembered her.

Mela still dreamed of her mother. The dreams were only half formed and elusive, as if her brain was desperately trying to fit the short memories and few pictures Mela still remembered into new sequences. Julie was always in her twenties in those dreams, even after Mela grew older than her mother had ever been. They left Mela with a sort of homesickness for her mother, an ache to know her better. She'd give everything to have one chance to talk with Julie adult to adult. She had so many questions.

Now that her balcony neighbor knew Julie, Mela was suddenly hesitant. A flood of unasked questions rose into her throat, stealing her voice.

But when would she be ready to find out more? In a year? In two? After thirty-seven years, did she truly need more time?

"What's the matter?" the old lady asked. "Am I wrong?"

"No," Mela said. "You're right. The bee lady was my mother."

There was no reply for a long time. The pause was so long Mela leaned against the wall and looked back out at the sea.

Maybe her neighbor had said all she wished to say on a gorgeous summer night. Maybe she was falling asleep. Despite the memories bubbling up like seafoam, despite the earlier upset at having been forgotten, Mela could see herself falling asleep as well. The waves were murmuring a song that soothed her like none other.

"Did you have dinner?" came suddenly a new question.

Mela turned back. "I've had some snacks."

"Would you like an apple? I have a bowl of apples."

"That's very kind of you, but I'm good. Is that what you ate for dinner? Apples?"

"No," the lady replied calmly. "I had coconut fried shrimp."

"That's nice," Mela said because she couldn't think of anything else to say.

Again there was a short silence. "No, I didn't have fried shrimp," the lady said sadly. "I had a cheese sandwich. It wasn't very good."

Down below in the garden, Peter cleared his throat. "It wasn't half bad," he said, his voice faceless in the night. "I put pickles and tomato on it because the doctor said to eat more vegetables."

"I don't like Swiss cheese," the lady said.

"You should've told me," Peter said. "Two years ago would've been good."

"Maybe you'll have something else tomorrow," Mela said. "Something you like better."

"Maybe." The lady fell silent again as if there wasn't much hope.

"I can get Gouda," Peter said. "Or Muenster."

Mela smiled, and then she yawned. "I need to charge my phone," she said. "Good night."

"Throw your phone away," was the only answer she got from her new neighbor.

Mela went back into her room, leaving the sliding door open so the night air could get in. Mela wished she could bottle the fragrance so she would always have it with her.

She had a charger in her purse and plugged her phone in, then went into the bathroom to rinse her mouth. After checking the soles of her feet, she rinsed those too.

If she was staying for a week, a whole seven days, she would have to get a change of clothes and a toothbrush. Other things too, probably. But all that was for the next day.

Mela pulled her sheet back and slipped into bed. For a moment, she considered switching on the TV to check if Rob had made it onto the news. There'd been critiques of his proposed tax policies that had some credit, and the opposition was making the most of it.

But it was too peaceful and quiet. Mela didn't want the news. For seven days, she wanted to press pause on her hectic life.

Mela snuggled into the pillow and closed her eyes. But even though she was tired and the waves rushed outside, she couldn't fall asleep.

She fished for her phone and pressed the power button.

Just one quick check for news.

CHAPTER 6

"Kimmie?" The voice sounded tired.

"Dad?" Pressing the phone to her ear, Kimmie pushed her duvet cover off and swung her legs out of bed. "What happened?"

It didn't take much to wake her. Her job as an investigative journalist had trained her to be up and running at a moment's notice.

"Everything is okay, Kimmie. I'm sorry for calling at this hour, but I just got back to the hotel."

"What's up? What's going on?" Kimmie glanced at the watch. It was two o'clock in the morning—never a time for good news.

"Your mom is in Bay Harbor."

"Bay Harbor? Aren't you in Concord?"

"I am." He cleared his throat. "Mom went to the bathroom just as we were taking off after a movie viewing, and the bus left without her."

"You left Mom at the theater?" Kimmie rubbed her forehead. Her parents' schedule was hectic enough for snags like this to happen, but the fact Dad called her about it was new. Her parents were immensely capable people who could deal with a wide range of situations. "Was Mom angry?"

"I don't know if she was angry," Dad admitted. "But for whatever reason, she decided not to come to where she was supposed to be. She went to her mother's house in Bay Harbor instead."

"Did she get her schedule mixed up?" Kimmie asked. Out of politeness, really. Mom hadn't mixed up her schedule; her feelings had been hurt.

"Must have."

"When did you notice she was missing?" Kimmie asked. "Right away? Did you send her a car?"

"Kimmie, I had back-to-back meetings all day," Dad said. "Johanna stood in for Mom."

Johanna, Mom's assistant. Kimmie's age, gorgeous, and a little too eager to please for Kimmie's taste. She frowned. "So when *did* you notice, Dad? Asking for a friend."

He sighed. "Oh, I don't know. I think she sent me a text or called or something. I couldn't make sense of it. I assumed she had other appointments to go to. Johanna is in charge of these things."

"Okay. Well, did she have an appointment in Bay Harbor then?"

"You'd have to ask your mother."

Mom told Dad if she left for the supermarket. She always did her best to stay connected, no matter how busy things got. Kimmie cleared her throat diplomatically. "I think she's ditched you, Daddy dearest."

"I have no idea what's going on," Dad said. "Listen, sweetheart, it's late. Are you on a job?"

"I just wrapped the last one." Kimmie went to the window to look outside. "Please don't remind me." She would forever remember the photos she took, the haunted eyes, the stories worming their way into her nightmares.

"I thought maybe you could go see Mom," Dad said. "Find out when she's coming back."

"Go to Mom's house in Bay Harbor?"

"That's right. Mom might have had it in her head to check on it. I don't know. I don't want to send any of my people in case—well, in case Mom's unwell. We don't need bad press right now."

Dad never needed bad press. Kimmie swallowed a sigh. Her entire childhood had been defined by the need to perform so there wouldn't be any bad news burdening him. "Okay. Sure. I can... Where exactly *is* Bay Harbor?"

"Uh...it's at the Maine coast near Camden, I believe. Just check your GPS, Kimmie. I don't know where she keeps the address, but you can text her."

"What if she doesn't answer?"

"As far as I know, the town is tiny. You'll find her. Tell her she needs to be at the ski resort day after tomorrow. It's a big benefit gala that will get a lot of attention in the media, and I can't very well open the dance floor with Johanna."

Kimmie frowned. She was standing by the window in her silk PJ's, looking out over the glittering city that never slept. As if to prove it, a group of pedestrians scurried along the sidewalks far below. "No, don't open the ball with Johanna," she said. "That would be weird."

"Well, one way or another I'll need someone," he said. "All right, Kimmie, let me know how it goes. I'd better catch an hour of sleep. I was told we'd be at it bright and early tomorrow."

"Good night, Dad."

Kimmie dialed Mom, going directly to voice mail. "It's me, Kimmie," she said. "Dad just called. He sounds confused about you leaving, Mom, and he wants me to meet you. Well, I hope you're still in Bay Harbor. I'll try and find it on a map. So call me back when you wake up, please. Maybe switch on your phone? People are trying to reach you. Love you. Bye."

For a while, Kimmie stayed by the window, looking into the night and thinking about her parents, marriage, Johanna.

Life was never easy, was it?

She considered going back to bed. But the side where Travis used to sleep was painfully empty. She wasn't yet thirty, and already, she'd lost herself a husband.

Her parents were in their late forties.

Dad was too busy to keep track of things, including his marriage. Of course it was Mom who kept it together.

She went into the kitchen and pulled the container with the leftover Thai green curry from the fridge, spooning a portion on a plate and microwaving it. Then she sat on the sofa and switched on the TV, skipping the news and stopping at a documentary about the sugar cane industry.

When she was done eating, she checked her phone. She didn't often talk with Mom. Between their combined schedules, a few minutes once a month was usually all they managed. Kimmie gave a fleeting thought to her siblings. Maybe she should text them to keep them in the loop?

She was even less in touch with her sister Sisley than she was with Mom and hardly ever talked to her brother Morris. Maybe once or twice a year, if they happened to run into each other at Christmas. Often enough, Morris ditched the family, preferring his newest girlfriend to tradition. Also, maybe Kimmie had argued with Sis last time they met. She couldn't remember.

She texted both of them anyway, feeling like a fool for staying in touch. She'd probably get no response at all from Morris, and Sisley would only get back to complain about her life.

Kimmie read a couple of emails praising her latest article and asking her to take on a new assignment. One was from a competing newspaper, and she marked it as important. She might check in with them and see what they had for her and how much they offered to pay. New York wasn't at its best in the middle of July. The sidewalks smelled, the streets were crowded with tourists, and the humidity was high enough to warrant a swimsuit instead of a suit.

Maybe going to the coast of Maine wasn't so bad. They had once been to Acadia National Park before Dad had turned to politics. Kimmie remembered piers and outlook points high above the sea, a scattering of tiny islands, and the bustling seaside town of Bar Harbor.

Almost the same as Bay Harbor.

For the longest time, Kimmie had thought the majestic hotel they'd stayed in belonged to Mom.

She smiled. She'd forgotten about that. When Mom had told her she owned a small house in a town called Bay Harbor instead of a hotel in Bar Harbor, Kimmie had cried.

She'd never been to Mom's house.

Yes, maybe she'd enjoy a couple of days at the coast of Maine. She knew next to nothing about her grandmother Julie, only that she'd drowned in a sailing accident. Mom never talked about it.

"Oh, Dad," Kimmie whispered and brought the empty curry plate into the kitchen to rinse it. Mom had a kind soul under her professional veneer, but she wasn't easily talked out of something she'd set her mind on.

Kimmie had a feeling that if she accepted Dad's assignment, she would have her work cut out for her.

CHAPTER 7

The golden light streaming through the glass balcony doors woke Mela. She blinked and struggled into an upright position. Why hadn't Johanna...

"Oh goodness," she whispered and rubbed her face. She was in Bay Harbor. She'd run away because Rob hadn't remembered to keep track of her. She'd behaved like a naughty four-year-old.

"Shoot," Mela said, louder now. Her heart started to hammer as guilt came crashing down on her. In a panic, she snatched up her phone. It wasn't even on! She'd accidentally yanked it off the charger leaving the newscast running until the battery had died again.

Mela hooked up the power, pressed the power button, and jumped out of bed, grabbing the remote from the TV and switching that on, too. She found the news, then checked her messages.

Johanna had texted to ask when she'd be back and what to do about appointments. Rob wasn't on the news. A quick google search brought up some photos at the mayor's reception. Johanna was standing between Rob and the mayor looking a little stressed.

Mela rubbed her hands over her face. Then she texted Johanna to cancel her appointments for the week. Last, she called Rob, but the call went to voice mail and she didn't feel like leaving a message.

She put down the phone, closed her eyes, and took a few moments to center herself.

It sort of felt okay, she thought. Like she still wasn't missed.

And she did need to do something about the house before it fell apart entirely. If rain had been getting in through the broken window, it had probably caused all sorts of damage.

Mela took a quick shower and then, unwilling to put the slept-in T-shirt back on, she dressed in her blouse and suit from yesterday, omitting the pantyhose. A quick twist of hair and a few bobby pins to finish the look, then she slipped her feet into her flip-flops, took her purse in one hand and her heels in the other, and left the room.

"Good morning." Peter was behind the reception counter, a newspaper spread out in front of him and a steaming mug waiting by his hand.

"Good morning." Mela put her purse on the counter.

"I like the shoe situation," Peter said and nodded appreciatively at the heels she was holding. "Can I get you a coffee? I also have bagels, cream cheese, and strawberries."

"Yes please to all," Mela said. "Thank you."

Peter pulled a mug out from under the counter as if it were a bar and went to fill it at the coffee urn beside the door.

"There you go for starters." He placed it in front of her and returned to his spot.

"Anything interesting in the newspaper?" Mela sipped her drink with appreciation.

Peter glanced at her. "Nothing about your husband. Lobster is cheap this summer."

"Yes, I heard." It was cheap because the lobster industry was in trouble. They needed help. Everybody needed help. Mela sipped again. "This is *really* good," she said.

"Don't sound so surprised." The laugh lines of his eyes crinkled though he didn't look up.

"I don't. I sound grateful." She set down her mug. "Listen, is there a car rental place nearby? I need to go shopping for something beachier than this." She nodded at her suit.

"Oh. I thought you had changed your mind and were ready to leave us again." He straightened and put his hands on the counter. "Which would be bad."

"You left too," she reminded him. "You went all the way to Africa to shoot cheetahs."

"With a camera," he said.

"With a camera," she confirmed. "That's what I meant."

There was a pause where they looked at each other.

"What are we talking about again?" he asked distractedly.

"I need a car," she explained, suppressing a laugh. "Because I need to go buy more appropriate clothes."

"Right. Well, there's a rental place close to Bay Port University. It's a bit of a drive, but I can bring you. They're expensive, though."

"That's all right."

"Or..." He chewed the inside corner of his lips. "Or you can rent my car. I'm expensive too, but at least I'm in town." He leaned on his forearms on the counter, grinning at her.

Again, Mela had to smile. "Your egg bike? Um, thank you. I think I'd better—"

"My pickup truck. It's great."

"A truck? I don't know. I was thinking of something smaller."

"You can put all the things you need to fix your house in the back," said Peter. "It's very useful."

It was true that Mela might as well give the money to Peter instead of a chain rental. "Sure," she agreed. "What about insurance and all that?"

"I'll take care of it. No worries."

"Okay."

"When do you need it?"

"As soon as I've had breakfast," she said. "I'm starving."

"You haven't had dinner." He nodded knowingly. "I heard you talking with Sunny last night."

"Is that my neighbor's name?" Mela drained her cup, and without asking, Peter took it and refilled it.

"Yes, that's her name. Sunny Gardiner."

"Does she live here?" Mela asked.

"Yes, she does." He tilted his head. "A couple of years ago, they had a landslide near the bird watching tower in Sandville," he said. "An entire cliff went crashing into the sea, and Sunny's house barely escaped the same fate. It's butting on the new edge and can slide into the ocean at any moment. Luckily, she was able to get out. But it's too dangerous to go back in and get her things, and she obviously can't sell the house, either."

It didn't take Mela long to put the pieces together. "She lost everything, and you took her in."

He shook his head, but when he noticed her eyes on him, he smiled as if she'd caught him out. "You could say I snapped her up cheap. She folds the motel towels for me, and I keep her away from fried foods like the doctor prescribed."

"Sounds like it's working out for both of you," Mela said, thinking that the world needed more people like Peter. "By the way, the room is great."

"Glad you like it." He closed the newspaper. "Did you know Sunny?"

"Because she knew my mother?" Mela shook her head. "I couldn't see her face last night. Maybe I'll remember her once I see her."

"It's been a long time, forty years, isn't it?"

"Yes. It was a different life."

"For me, too. Coming back here after working abroad was an adjustment." Wistfully, Peter looked over her head. "To say the least."

Mela would have liked to know what he meant by that. Maybe she could ask in a few days when they knew each other better. She cleared her throat. "But the sea is nice, isn't it? I can't be the only one who loves it."

"The sea is very nice." His gaze returned to her. "I came back here because it was my grandfather who built the motel. The night of his fortieth birthday, he dreamed an old fisherman told him to sell his lobster boat and build a place for people to stay in Bay Harbor. Who am I to defy my grandfather's dream fisherman? Gramps would haunt me to the ends of Africa if I didn't keep the motel open and running."

Mela didn't miss the crease that had appeared between his eyes. Had it really only been his grandfather who'd had a dream?

"I'm very glad you do keep the place open," she said. "I, for one, would've had an uncomfortable night otherwise." And Sunny probably had no other place to stay at all.

Suddenly, Mela's stomach growled. She pressed a hand to it. "Would you like to join me for breakfast, Peter?"

"Sure. And then I'll show you the truck." He pointed at a door behind Mela. "Breakfast is right through there. I'll be there in a moment."

"Okay." Mela took her coffee through to the small breakfast room. There was a table with cereals and milk, the promised bagels, a plate of iced grapes, and small bowls of blueberries and strawberries. She helped herself, cutting open a sesame bagel and pushing it into a toaster. The window looked out at the street. The already sun-drenched sidewalk was empty.

"Almost as if everyone else is also still at home, having a nice breakfast," she murmured to herself. "Whatever happened to racing out the door with a protein shake in hand?"

"Don't expect to see much of that." Peter had come in. He took a plate and started filling it too. "The tempo in Bay Harbor is a bit slower than elsewhere. And by a bit, I mean a whole lot."

"I'd like to slow down." Mela dropped a dollop of whipped cream cheese on her plate. "My tempo has been set to crazy for decades. Every year, time seems to speed up."

She picked a table by the window, and Peter sat with her, bringing a toasted bagel and a bowl of blueberries.

"Isn't that exhausting?" he asked. "Always being on the run?"

Mela shrugged. "I'm used to it," she said diplomatically. "But I do need to fix up Mom's house. Are there good contractors in the area?"

"There are a few. I can give you a number if you tell me what you need."

"I'll let you know when I've taken stock. I do know there's a broken window."

"Do you want me to have a look?"

"Oh." Mela blinked. "Uh." Was it too much to say yes, please? She already stayed in Peter's motel and was going to use his truck. Maybe it was too much. Running off to take a break was one thing. Being photographed twice with the same handsome man who wasn't her husband was a different thing. "Thanks very much. Maybe later," Mela said politely. "Right now, I have to go buy clothes." She stood, taking her plate and mug to the dish bin by the buffet table and putting them inside. "Thank you for breakfast, Peter."

He stood as well, clearing away his plate and mug. "Let me get you the truck, and then I'll be out of your hair."

CHAPTER 8

Amelie pushed a short curl behind her ear. Now that she was standing in front of the motel, she felt silly. Pamela hadn't been in touch once since she'd left Bay Harbor.

The day Julie and Finn Palmer had gone sailing, Mela had stayed at Amelie's. She'd been in a terrible state when it became clear, long after the sun had gone down, that the boat wasn't coming back. Not that night, and maybe never.

Amelie remembered holding her friend as she sobbed, the two of them tucked into her pink canopy bed while the adults waited by the phone. She'd been in shock herself because she'd adored Julie. Also, she'd never before seen Mela cry. Not once. It had terrified Amelie to see tears stream from her friend's eyes like water from a faucet. All her little girl brain could hold on to was that she needed to hold her best friend.

The next morning, Grandma had come and picked up Amelie for a day of pony rides and peach pie at the county fair. Mom had waved from the door, holding Mela in her arms, even though she was much too big to be carried. Mela's face had been buried in Mom's shoulder.

Amelie cried her way through the stupid fair, and when Grandma finally drove her back home, Mela hadn't been there anymore. As far as Amelie knew, her childhood friend had never been back to Bay Harbor. The entire thing had been traumatic, and all the pony rides and pies in the world couldn't help that Amelie had lost her two favorite people.

Amelie still wondered whether Mom should've kept Mela. Even if it would've meant more nights of Amelie suffering alongside her scared friend, her arms wrapped around Mela's shaking shoulders, her night-gown wet from the tears.

But since that time, Amelie had raised a son herself and it had softened the edge of her doubts. Maybe she would have done the same to protect her child. It was one of the many calls each parent had to make on their own when there was no clear right or wrong.

Then, one day, Mela had shown up on TV, blond and skinny and smiling a fixed smile at the side of her politician husband.

That, too, had been a bit of a shock.

Amelie wrapped her arms around herself because she was cold even though the temperature had already risen into the low eighties.

Nothing gained, nothing lost.

She went to the door and lifted her hand. Before her knuckles hit the wood, the door opened and there stood Mela.

Amelie stepped back.

Mela was dressed the same as she was on TV. Only she was wearing hot pink flip-flops and carried her TV heels in her hand.

Peter appeared behind Mela. When he saw Amelie, he faded back into the darkness of the room.

"Hi," Amelie said and tucked the curl back again.

"Hello," Mela replied. She looked confused.

"Do you remember me?" Amelie smiled tentatively.

"Amelie?" Mela came outside, the shells crunching under her sandals. She smelled of coffee and, faintly, Peter's lemon soap. "Amelie Cobb," Mela said. "It's you!"

"Pamela." Amelie wanted to hug Mela, but their friendship had been too long ago. She held out her hand, feeling awkward.

"Oh." Mela took her hand and gave it a light squeeze. "It's still Mela."

"Peter said you were staying here," Amelie explained, glad that it was still Mela. "Otherwise I would have—I thought maybe you'd want—"

Mela shook her head once as if to clear her thoughts. "Goodness, Amelie, I think of you all the time. I can't believe you're here. Look at you!"

"Forty years older, eh?" Mela herself looked fantastic, but Amelie had already known that.

"Can I give you a hug?" Mela asked.

"Yes," Amelie said. Mela's face was different than the one she'd seen on TV. There was no fixed smile. It was still the same face, more mature now, that had cried on little Amelie's shoulder back then.

Mela dropped her heels to the ground and hugged Amelie, and Amelie returned the embrace, and suddenly it was her crying on Mela's shoulder.

"Are you two okay out here?" Peter came outside to join them.

They broke apart, both wiping their eyes and smiling, a little embarrassed.

"Yes, all good. Thanks for texting me, Peter," Amelie said. If he hadn't, she and Mela might've missed each other.

"Sure."

"How's Sunny?"

"Sleeping late as usual. Mela wants to buy some things. Could you show her where the shops are?"

"I'd love to." Amelie turned to Mela. "Where would you like to go?"

"I need clothes." Mela spread her arms to show her immaculate suit. "I want to get out of this asap. I'm already starting to sweat."

"We have a couple of nice little boutiques in Bay Harbor," Amelie said. "But if you want something high end, we should go to Sandville."

"The local boutiques, please," Mela said. "The closer, the better."

"She's only staying for a week," Peter explained. "I'm going to bring you the truck."

"Oh, she's getting the truck?" Amelie raised an inquiring eyebrow.

"Yep." He walked off.

"I didn't drive my car," Mela explained. "Coming here was kind of a...uh. A spontaneous decision." A frown flew across her face, gone before it settled.

"It's good you came," Amelie said. "Your house needs a bit of TLC. I almost went in to fix it, but you know... I wasn't sure."

"I thought there was a company supposed to take care of the house," Mela said. "Maybe the contract expired? How long has the kitchen window been broken?"

"A few weeks, I think. We had a little rain, but mostly it's been dry."

A horn squawked, and they both turned to the street. Parked on the curb stood Peter's blue truck.

"What is that?" Mela asked weakly.

Amelie smiled. "I think that's the 1939 Chevrolet half-ton."

Peter jumped out of the truck, slammed the door shut, and strode to meet them. He dangled a key at Mela, and she took it. "Treat her well," he said. "She takes regular."

"What regular?" Mela looked confused again.

"Regular gas. Don't try and put premium gas in the tank; she won't like it."

"Peter..." Mela took a deep breath. "Are you sure I should be driving an antique truck?"

"I like to call her vintage. She's not *that* old."

"It's fine, Mela," Amelie said, trying not to laugh at her friend's expression. "Come on, let's go."

Peter walked off, hands pushed in the pockets of his jeans, and Mela went with Amelie to the truck.

"He picked me up with a motorbike yesterday," Mela said as she opened the driver's door. The handle stuck, but she managed to yank it open.

"Maybe he likes you." Amelie climbed into the passenger seat. She cranked the window down, which was harder than she expected, and rested her arm on the frame. "He doesn't share his toys with everyone."

"I'm honored. I also hope this isn't... What *is* that?" She touched a lever.

Amelie had no idea either. "Can you drive stick?"

"Maybe? Where is the clutch? This one?"

They laughed. It took them a few minutes to figure out what the levers and knobs were, but once they did, Mela managed to put the truck in gear and drive off.

"Left at the light." Amelie held her face into the sweet breeze. "Listen, you've been in town for all of five minutes, and I've already had more fun today than the rest of the week."

Mela held out her pinkie finger.

Without thinking, Amelie leaned over and, for a moment, hooked it with her own. It was ages since they'd last done that. It felt strangely intimate.

"I'm glad you stopped by the motel," Mela said. "I always wondered what happened back then."

A car honked behind them, the horn going again and again.

"What's wrong? What did I do?" Mela peered into the mirror.

"Nothing, I think." Amelie twisted to look back. "He's waving. I think he just likes your ride." She held a hand out the window and waved back, and the honker passed them, grinning and yelling something they couldn't understand over the noise of their engine.

Mela let out an audible breath. "Let's go find a place where they have mimosas. What do you think?"

"The shops aren't even open yet," Amelie agreed. "And I do know a little bistro by the sea that makes good mimosas. I'm here for it."

Another car honked its driver's appreciation behind them, and they giggled.

Amelie navigated them to the beach where the bistro was, and Mela parked.

Forty years older or not, Amelie thought as she climbed onto the sand and kicked off her sandals to carry them. She was ready to find out whether Mela was still her friend.

CHAPTER 9

Mela lifted her orange juice prosecco and drank. Her feet were buried in the sand that was still warm from the day before. There was no wind, and the water reflected the sky's unbroken blue like shimmering glass. If only life could always be this easy, she thought.

"I knew it was beautiful here," she told Amelie. "But it's even better. It's real."

"Real?"

Mela nodded. "In a corner of my mind, I was always afraid I was being nostalgic. That it wasn't as good as I remembered."

The waiter brought a basket with butter croissants and portion packets of butter and jam. Mela chose apricot, and Amelie picked blueberry.

"Sometimes I start watching an old movie I used to love," Amelie said, scooping a bit of jam with a piece of croissant. "Only to find after a few minutes that it's different from what I thought it was. Like that?"

"Yes," Mela said and took another sip. "Exactly like that. You still understand me, Amelie."

"And yet we barely know each other. Isn't that weird?"

"It is. It's... We need to change that." Mela had only one week in Bay Harbor. She badly wanted to fix a house, a friendship, and, ideally, an old motel. It would be a shame if it went out of business since there was no other place to put up tourists.

"Let's change it," Amelie agreed, pulling Mela out of her thoughts. "Where do we start?"

Mela set her glass down. "First things first, I suppose. We need to catch up. Do you have kids?"

"Yes." Amelie drained her drink. "I have a son."

"Uh-oh." Mela laughed. "Is he trouble? What's his name?"

"His name is Bennett."

"Bennett. Should I ask about the rest?"

Ten or so years ago, Amelie's parents had sold their Portland pastry shops to a big chain, and the sales price had been so eye-wateringly high it made the news. Amelie had been the only child of doting parents, even if her mother Meredith had been quite different from Julie. Mela had always assumed Amelie would have a great life.

Now it sounded like she had a son with a criminal history.

But Amelie chuckled. "I love him to bits. He's stubborn. That's it."

Mela smiled. "Stubbornness is a good trait in my book. How old is he?"

"He's about to turn twenty-nine," Amelie said. "I had him young."

The math wasn't hard to do. Mela and Amelie were the same age, so she'd had her son at eighteen. "I'm only two years behind with my oldest," Mela said. "What's your husband's name?"

Amelie lifted her hand. There was no ring on her finger. "I'm flying solo." She tore off another piece of croissant and crumbled it between her fingertips. "Bennett wasn't exactly planned."

Mela nodded, though it was the last thing she'd expected. Between the two of them, Amelie had always been the good one, the one whose parents had her life all mapped out. Even as a child, Mela had known that.

"That can't have been easy," Mela said, feeling her way forward. "I remember your mom, and I know she wanted the best for you. I imagine she was worried."

Amelie widened her eyes. "Worried is the understatement of the century." She picked up her latte bowl and sipped. "I was determined to have the baby. Once we settled that, she made the best of it." She sighed. "To be honest, if Bennett would've come to me with news of becoming a dad at eighteen, I might've needed a moment myself."

Mela laughed quietly at Amelie's expression. "Having kids yourself changes how you see your mother, doesn't it?"

"Hush." Amelie grinned. "Well, *now* I wouldn't mind if Bennett would get a move on." She set her bowl back on the wobbly bistro table. "I wish he would find someone nice, to tell you the truth." She shook her head. "I've become *that* mom."

"I understand completely," Mela said. "My oldest just got divorced. I wish she would have been spared that. I think she's lonely, and I also think she's in danger of putting up walls to protect herself. But they're still young, Amelie. They'll work it out." She hoped.

"It's never straightforward," Amelie agreed. "On top of it all, Bennett has the worst job in the world for settling down."

"Which is?"

"He's a detective," Amelie said. "He's in Cape Bass right now, but he wants to get a job here as soon as he can. The Cape is getting too crowded for his taste, and he doesn't like it when I call him Cape Cop Cobb. He's very..." She thought. "Very *proper*. Even as a little boy, everything always had to be just so. It drove me nuts because it reminded me so much of Mom. I was afraid he'd turn out like her." She smiled. "It's all good now. I tease him, but I'm enormously proud."

"Your son is a detective." Mela shook her head in amazement. "Goodness, Amelie, who'd have thought?"

"And you?"

"You might've seen mine on TV," Mela said. "Kimmie's my oldest at twenty-eight. She's an investigative journalist. Sisley is my youngest, and Morris is in the middle. He's a pianist."

"Wow. Very impressive."

"If I'm honest, it's hard." Mela looked at her friend. She'd never admitted this to anyone. "I worry Kimmie will get hurt, I worry Sisley isn't happy, and I worry Morris doesn't take anything seriously." She sighed. "Frankly, I was glad to have nannies to help me raise them. Now I feel guilty that I didn't do it all myself. Maybe they didn't get enough mom time."

Amelie patted Mela's hand. "There's no one right way of doing it," she assured her. "Also, there's time to straighten the ship. Cape Cop Cobb and I talk at least once a month, though half the time we're arguing. It's all done with goodwill, of course."

Mela chuckled. "I should probably call them more often," she said. "I barely ever have time to just ask how they are."

"They might like that," Amelie said. "And the best thing is, you can start today."

"Uh. Maybe." Mela blinked. "Oh goodness, Amelie," she blurted out. "I don't *want* to call them. I'm a terrible mother."

"Maybe you're a little scared you won't be able to make them as happy as you want them to be," Amelie said. "I wouldn't be surprised, after what happened to you."

Mela inhaled the clean air. "Let's talk about something else. What do you do?"

"I'm a psychologist." Amelie looked out at the water. "What else could I become? Losing Julie and you, being raised by a demanding mother and an absent father, turned me into a proper basket case. I went to therapy until I knew enough to *be* the therapist." Now that Amelie was more relaxed, she seemed more confident in herself. "What about you?" Amelie asked. "You're famous."

"Am I?" Mela frowned. Not to her knowledge.

"Aren't you? Almost the governor's wife, the first lady of New Hampshire."

"Well," Mela said. "Rob is the one that counts."

Amelie glanced at her. "I hear your support does a lot of heavy lifting."

Mela sighed. "I want people to have a shot at a good life. That's what's important. Nothing else. Least of all fame. I honestly don't want it."

"But you're important too," Amelie said after a short pause. "Don't you think?"

Mela shrugged. "Who am I to make it about myself?"

Amelie put a hand on the table, almost as if she was reaching for Mela. "When I started working, I thought the same thing," she said after a while. "I thought my purpose in this world was to serve others. I don't believe that anymore."

"Then what do you believe instead?"

Amelie held her face into the sun. "I get to just be. I get to enjoy my life. I get to help others too, but I don't have to do it all the time."

"Oh. Well, I have my selfish moments. Like, right now."

"Is it selfish to have breakfast with a friend? I think living our lives for ourselves makes us happier. And when we're happy, we make others happy."

It sounded nice. But Mela thought that maybe it was too simple a concept. What about the kids experiencing food insecurity? Who cared about Mela being happy while an eight-year-old was too hungry to focus in school?

Mela stood. "I'm boiling," she said, fanning her silk blouse away from her skin. "I'll be back in a second."

"Don't go in to pay," Amelie said. "Breakfast is on me."

Mela smiled and went inside. There was a tiny but clean bathroom in the back, and she dabbed her face with cold water. The suit wasn't meant for the beach.

On the way out, she stopped the waiter carrying their check and paid before she went back outside, showing her wallet to Amelie as a sign they were good to go.

Amelie shook her head and tucked her wallet back. "Next one's on me," she said. "At least this way, I get to take you for a repeat."

"Shall we go to the boutique?" Mela asked. "Preferably one that sells swimsuits. I can't wait to get in the water."

Amelie stood. "I haven't swum in years," she said. "Funny thing about living in a beach town is that you stop going to the beach."

"Why?" Mela faced the water and spread her arms as if she wanted to embrace the sea. "It's glorious."

Amelie stepped beside her. "I come up with all sorts of reasons, but if I'm honest, I just don't want to go on my own. Also, I'm too big." She wrapped her arms around herself. "I don't like flopping around in a swimsuit. I'd rather stay away from the beach than feel people judge me. And when I say people, I know I mostly mean me."

"Some psychologist you are." Mela hooked her arm under Amelie's. "I think we might need to buy two swimsuits today, because tomorrow, you're in the water with me. Nobody cares how we look. There aren't even that many people on the beach."

"I care how I look."

"So are you judging how others look as well?"

"No, just myself. I love seeing people feel good in their skin, and it doesn't matter to me how big or skinny they are. I love happy energy."

"If you judge yourself, you must do it to others too, my dear."

Gently arguing the point back and forth, they slowly made their way back to the vintage pickup truck.

"Don't count on me joining you," Amelie summarized as she brushed the sand off her feet and slipped her sandals back on. "But let's go see what we can find in the swimsuit department."

CHAPTER 10

Driving the truck was as much an adventure as before. Amelie directed, and Mela tried to divide her attention between the light traffic and the quaint stores tempting shoppers with decorated windows and cute hand-painted signs. For years, Mela had outsourced her shopping. She couldn't wait to park and start visiting the pretty displays she glimpsed.

The first boutique had shelves of brightly colored knits and linen clothes, displays of locally crafted pearl and silver jewelry, and a satisfying selection of straw hats and fluttery summer scarves. Mela found loose tunics and linen pants she liked as well as a flowing white dress she fell in love with the moment she spotted it. In the back of the store, she spotted underwear and silky slips that felt like spun air on her skin and would double as nightgowns. On the way out, she spotted a pair of pretty summer wedges to go with her new clothes and bought them as well.

The next stop was a local drugstore that smelled of eucalyptus and bath salts. Amelie went to find multivitamins for her son and violet pastilles for herself, and

Mela purchased a toothbrush and paste, floss, soap, a brush, and a small bottle of sun lotion.

In the second clothing store, they found cheerful swimsuits with clever ruching to slim a nice, comfortable tummy. Expensive as they were, Amelie bought one without needing further prodding.

Delighted with her friend's courageous purchase, Mela bought Amelie a second suit as a thank-you gift for taking her shopping, and then she bought herself a simple black suit and a pair of elegant sunglasses that made her feel like a Cote D'Azur beach beauty from the fifties.

"Goes with the truck," she said contently as the saleslady wrapped the glasses in silk paper and stowed them together with the suit in a pretty paper bag. "And also my age. I'm almost fifty."

"Not so fast," Amelie said, peering at the suits in her own bag. One was cherry red, the other one canary yellow. "We still have a couple of years before we hit that milestone. We have to draw time out and enjoy it as much as we can."

Smiling, Mela ran her credit card. "It's not going to feel different after you turn fifty. But sure. We should enjoy every day as much as we possibly can."

Amelie closed her bag dramatically and sighed. "I'll never be able to pull these colors off. I thought you'd buy the hot pink one for yourself. You left me hanging."

Mela shook her head. If the press caught her in a pink swimsuit and ditching her duties, the internet comments would be relentless. "You look gorgeous, my dear. Unlike me, you have the tan and the curves to pull bright colors off. I'm not going to steal your thunder."

"Thunder *thighs*, maybe," Amelie murmured, but Mela saw her sneak another happy peek at the new suits.

"I bought the polka-dotted one," the saleslady chimed in. "I also thought I didn't have the figure for it, but it makes me so happy to wear it."

Amelie laughed. "That's the important bit, I suppose."

Next, they drove to the supermarket where Amelie bought plum purée to use instead of butter in her baking. Mela bought apples and grapes, bread and a variety of cheeses, a bottle of white and a bottle of red wine, a gorgeous bunch of tulips, and a couple of beach towels from the seasonal aisle. Then they returned to Julie's house, and Mela parked.

"Oh Mela," Amelie said quietly, looking at the poor state of the house.

"I really should sell it," Mela said just as softly.

"No, you have to keep it. You don't need the money, do you?"

Mela shook her head. "But it deserves a family with kids who love it as much as I did. And a family deserves that gorgeous oceanfront property."

"I wish I could buy it," Amelie said, a note of panic in her voice. "But..." She shrugged. "Otherwise someone from Boston or New York City will snap it up and tear it down so they can put in a modern bungalow they visit twice a year."

"In Bay Harbor? Hardly." Still, the thought made Mela's heart and stomach turn. "Let's go in," she suggested. "I've just come back. I don't want to think about the future yet."

Amelie glanced at her as she opened her door. "Everything okay with you and Robert?" she asked casually.

Mela had told her some about what had happened, but not all. It was for her and Robert to work things out between themselves.

They climbed out and walked up the short path. "Mom had roses in that spot," Mela pointed to avoid the question about the state of her marriage. "Looks like they're gone now. I might get new ones."

Again Amelie glanced at her, but she let it go.

Mela unlocked the door and entered the house for the second time. At her side, like so many times in the past, was her friend.

"It looks almost the same as I remember," Amelie said.

"After they took me away, someone came to clean up," Mela said. She led the way into the kitchen. "I know there was food in the fridge and plates in the sink when I left. My foster parents told me it'd all be taken care of, but I worried about it. I didn't want people to come and take anything away." The memories came back one by one. "Like the packet of Reese's Pieces. I forgot! Mom had bought a bag as a special treat for me waiting for her all day. I'd begged her to let me try the candy because..." She tried to remember why it'd been such a big deal to her. “Right. Because that kid in the movie used Reese’s Pieces to lure E.T. out of hiding.”

“Oh, that movie was so sad.” Amelie smiled wistfully.

“It really was.” Mela opened the fridge and held her hand inside. “I called last night to restore utilities—hey, it’s cold! Great!” She put her cheese packets in the fridge. The fridge needed cleaning, but the cheese was wrapped in plastic, so it would be okay.

“Mela, there are don’t-use stickers on the toilets,” Amelie called out from wherever she’d gone while Mela put the groceries away. “I think the house is winterized so the pipes won’t burst.” She returned from the bathroom with a yellow sticker in hand.

“Yes, it should’ve been.” Mela dialed the number on the sticker, and a few minutes later, she was talking with a plumber who said he was in the neighborhood and could stop by to take out aerators and turn on valves so she had water.

“Should we open the windows to air out?” Amelie asked. “The dust is starting to make me sneeze.”

They went through the house, throwing open the windows and taking off the yellow stickers. Then the plumber came—a stroke of sheer good luck—and soon Mela and Amelie were flushing the toilets and opening faucets until the water ran clear. Finally, Mela filled a vase, put her tulips inside, and set it on the table.

And then, Mela sat on the dusty sofa and started crying.

"Uh-oh," Amelie said and sat beside her, rubbing her back. "It's all too much, isn't it? Julie always had flowers on the table too. It's so pretty."

"Sorry," Mela sobbed, hiding her face.

"Nonsense," Amelie said and stood. "Sit there and cry. It needs to come out. Who knows, I might join you too." She went into the kitchen, and Mela heard her rummage through the cabinets until she came back. "Here. Forty-year-old tissues. Hope *you* don't have a dust allergy."

Mela giggle-sobbed and pulled a wad of tissues from the box.

Amelie put it on the coffee table, and then she sat on the chair. "I feel ten years old again in here," she said after a while.

"Me too," Mela blew her nose. "That's why I'm crying."

"Did they ever find her?" Amelie asked after a short pause. "Mom kept it from me as much as she could, and I never found a mention on the internet."

Mela shook her head. "They never found her or Uncle Finn, or even the boat. There was nothing."

"That's hard."

"I think a small part of my brain still… I *still…*"

"Still hope?" Amelie helped out.

Mela nodded, and then she cried again, overwhelmed by the past streaming back like the wave that swallowed Julie in her dreams.

Eventually, the tears did their job. Feeling calmer, Mela stood.

"Better?" Amelie asked kindly.

Mela nodded gratefully. The crying hadn't made her friend uncomfortable. Amelie had simply sat with Mela, quietly providing the space Mela needed to stay with her feelings and ride out her confusion. Few people were able to do that.

"Thank you so much, Amelie. I'm sorry for hanging on to you so long—I'm sure you have plans for the day."

"Anytime, my dear." Amelie stood as well and came to hug Mela. "I do have to see a client tonight, and Bennett is coming over for dinner. I'll call a cab to pick me up, but I'd like to see you again before you leave."

"Me too," Mela said. "But I don't want to get on your nerves. I'm not asking you to hold my hand every day after forty years of being out of touch."

"Don't be silly. Besides, the tears are out now. You'll be okay."

Mela went to wash her face while Amelie called for a cab, and then they went to the door.

The sun and the flowers outside cheered the rest of the sorrow away. Mela picked a bouquet of small pink sweetheart roses and gave it to Amelie for her kitchen table.

"How does breakfast in the garden tomorrow morning sound? I'll bring mimosas and cleaning supplies," Amelie offered.

"Sounds like something a good friend would say," Mela said, relieved that Amelie truly didn't seem to have minded her tears or the difficult memories. "I'll be here, so come whenever you feel like it."

A red car with the words 'Beach Cab' painted on the door turned into the street and stopped by the curb. A young man was sitting behind the wheel, nodding hello.

Mela nodded back.

"Don't spend the night here," Amelie advised. "You won't sleep a wink thinking about Julie."

"I'll stay at the motel," Mela said. "I have a room for six more days."

Amelie went to the cab and opened the door. "Hi, thanks for coming, Greg," she greeted the driver, then looked back at Mela. "I meant to ask: have you met Sunny yet?"

"Only in passing. I heard she's a permanent motel guest."

"Peter takes care of her," Amelie said wistfully. "She can be a little crusty sometimes, but she's only protecting a sweet soul that has been through a lot. She's just as devoted to Peter as he is to her." She sat in the car and waved goodbye.

"I'll make sure to get to know her a little better tonight." Mela waved back, Amelie closed the door, and the cab set off.

Mela returned to the kitchen where she cleaned away the glass shards from the broken window. It didn't look like there was water damage; the window must've shattered sometime after the maintenance company's last check-in. Then Mela played a dance mix from the '80s on her phone and set to filling buckets and soaking sponges.

She couldn't restore the warmth and joy Julie had spread in the house. But at least she could make things better than they were now.

Mela took a deep breath, braced herself, and then she dove into dusting off, quite literally, the life she'd had to give up so long ago, wondering what she would find under the cobwebs.

CHAPTER 11

I love watching Mela play when she thinks she is alone. She'll grow up so fast. I already know that I will miss my baby too soon.

An hour after she started wiping off the dust, Mela was done. Not done cleaning but *done.*

It was too much. She caved. She couldn't do it all today. Everything she touched, everything she handled, was charged with the energy of her lost childhood, and it had become too much to handle.

Of course it was unfair. Bad things happened to good people all the time. Mela knew that. But when she felt drained like now, her brain refused to accept it.

How could Julie have lost her life so young? What gifts would she have given to the world had she lived?

What would Mela's own life have looked like?

She'd had good foster parents and even better adoptive parents. But she'd never stopped wondering how it would have been had Julie raised her.

In the end, Mela sat on Julie's bed and put a hand on the pillow. The cover was made, and she was sure Mom had never made her bed—so probably the social workers who'd cleaned the fridge and washed the dishes had gone through the house and emptied the wastebaskets, made the beds, and hung up scattered clothes.

But while Julie's bedspread was straight, her pillow was crooked.

Mela laid down on Mom's bed, pulling her legs up. And then, carefully, softly, she laid her face on her mother's pillow. For the time it took a dust mote to dance through a light beam or a pillow to exhale the past stored between its feathers, Mela thought she could smell Julie's scent.

Then it was gone.

Mela closed her eyes, and there was Julie. Smiling, holding out her hands, waiting.

For a long while, Mela lay on the bed, remembering her mother as best she could.

It wasn't much. If Mela was honest, she had trouble even seeing the details of her mother's face. She could recall only a small handful of expressions. A smile, a laugh, the distracted expression when Julie read or wrote, the focus while doing bee work.

There must have been a hundred expressions more.

Only Mela couldn't recall them. Even as a teenager, Mela had worried she would forget. The therapist had claimed it was normal. Some memories were lost to time, some to trauma, and eventually, Mela had stopped sharing her worries. She'd fed the therapist bits and pieces about made-up dreams and fears and the school stuff that seemed to worry her peers. It kept him busy and away from her real thoughts.

That and working hard had been good enough for survival. A little later, when Angela had allowed her to volunteer at a therapeutic riding center, Mela had discovered helping others. It made her feel useful. And being useful had finally seemed a good enough reason to keep going.

Mela changed position on Julie's bed. And then she moved again because something hard pressed against her cheekbone.

She rose on her elbows and slipped a hand under the pillow. There was a book... A thin booklet with a little lock.

Mela stared at the journal in her hand.

Julie's journal.

A new memory flooded back to Mela; one she'd never seen before. Julie was sitting beside her on the sofa, wearing a fluffy white sweater and jeans shorts, her hair in a fishtail braid. She was guiding Mela's hand over a paper, smiling when she let go. *You just wrote your first letter, sweetheart!*

Mela felt dizzy with the unexpected gift of the memory. She would come back to the look in Julie's eyes, the tone of her voice, the turn of her head. Now that the memory had come to her, it was hers to keep.

"Mom." Mela let her fingertips glide over the journal. "You're here, aren't you? You gave it to me."

There was no response other than the rushing of the sea outside the window and nothing else under the pillow or the thin duvet, nothing in the nightstand drawer or below the mattress. Suddenly, Mela felt she should go outside.

Clutching the journal, she skipped down the stairs almost as fast as if she were ten again. Mela yanked open the sliding patio door and jumped down the step. Only when she stood in the heat of the backyard did she stop and look around.

There were flowers everywhere. Julie had planted goldenrod and lavender for the bees, bee balm, and white wild indigo. Ferns and variegated hosta plants reigned in the shady spots under ancient magnolia trees and rhododendrons. The large flower beds Uncle Finn had edged with stones from the beach were crowded, with weeds growing companionably between perennials that had propagated themselves for years. The pretty, smooth stones were visible only here and there in the riot of colors and scents.

Behind the flower beds, guarded from wind and rain by an old stone wall, stood the beehives. Seven of them, because Julie had said it was a magical number and just enough to get started.

Three hives had toppled over, and the white paint had peeled off all of them, showing the weathered wood. It took work to maintain good hive boxes and...

Mela squinted.

A small brown dot launched itself from the entrance board of the middle hive. Another one, another one...and then a fourth dot suddenly dropped from the blue sky onto the entrance board and crawled busily inside.

"Well, hello there," Mela whispered and walked over for a closer look. She could see more bees launching and landing, fuzzy little foragers dressed in amber and yellow. The honeybees were focused only on bringing in nectar, zooming past her head without a second thought. Mela knew the colony needed to work hard to gather enough honey for the winter.

When Mela came so close she could touch the hive, two bees standing on the entrance board turned to face her, their forelegs raised, their wings lifted tersely above the striped rumps.

Julie had once told Mela that bees started their adult lives inside the hive, working their way through a succession of housekeeping jobs until they finally were old and smart enough to do the hardest and most challenging work of all: leaving the safety of home to find nectar. Guarding the hive entrance was the last job for a worker before becoming a forager. Driven by ancient instinct to ensure only their sweet-smelling sisters entered, guards simultaneously learned the sounds and scents and dangers of the world outside.

The last thing Mela remembered was that all honeybees were willing to sacrifice themselves so the colony might live. Foragers were both too distracted and valuable to do it lightly, and it took squashing them to get stung. But when a guard bee looked at you sideways, it was time to back away. The tiny bouncers didn't hesitate to die for the fame and glory of defending the house.

Mela took a couple of steps backward. The guards relaxed, setting their tiny feet back on the board, and turned to check out a bee that had just landed. Mela smiled.

She'd not thought much about honeybees for ages. But it was good to know her fondness for them was alive and well. She knew as much about them as any other pets she'd had; their little tasks, rewards and worries, and the colony's machinations that let thousands and thousands of individuals live together more peacefully and prosperously than any humans could ever do.

Maybe that was why Julie had loved the bees. She'd wanted harmony and often talked about ways to create it. Mela herself, older and more experienced in the ways of the world, had more pragmatic hopes for people.

A new honeybee launched, and this one was much bigger and fuzzier, with huge eyes—a drone. It slowly flew toward her. Mela snatched it from the air, feeling it buzz in her fist. When it settled, she opened her hand and looked at the little fellow sitting in her hand. She petted its thick fur with the tip of her finger as if it were a winged teddy bear.

Colonies raised drones only a few times each year because the males' sole task was to woo virgin queens into airborne romance. Afterward, their sisters closed ranks and cut their stingless brothers off, leaving them to die the cheerless death of the useless.

It was pretty rough.

Mela pursed her lips and gently blew until the drone spread his wings and left. She sat down on the kitchen step, on the side where she'd always sat. Then she put her mother's journal on her knees and pulled a bobby pin from her pocket to crack the tiny lock.

Chapter 12

Kimmie parked her car in the supermarket lot in Sandville and got out. It was hotter than she'd expected, even though it was already going on five, but the air was pleasantly dry and a light sea breeze made for an altogether gorgeous afternoon. She slipped off her black suit jacket and tossed it on the passenger seat. Then she pushed up her mirrored aviators and pulled up the map on her phone.

The town had beautiful beaches, but she still had another half hour of driving ahead of her. Bay Harbor truly was at the end of the world. Kimmie had traveled to remote villages in Afghanistan and felt more in the midst of things than here.

She stretched and leaned on her Audi convertible. A woman pushed a grocery cart out of the market, coaxing two small kids in matching shorts along. That was it. Nothing else was happening.

Kind of peaceful, Kimmie suddenly thought. Maybe the mother and her babies would go home and glue pasta pictures. Was that still a thing? Mom had tried to do family activities like that when they were young.

They usually ended with Sisley whining, Morris throwing a fit, or her becoming bored and slipping away.

She slipped her aviators back on her nose and ran a hand through her jet-black pixie cut.

Mom had never gotten over her mother's death. But to ditch Dad during the bus tour and just take off? That wasn't like Mom. That wasn't like Mom at all. She'd probably been the one organizing the bus tour in the first place.

Kimmie shook the thought of Johanna from her brain and considered going into the market to buy a soda. But then she got back into her Audi and pulled back onto the street.

After a couple of turns, she got trapped behind a biker. Not one in fancy Lycra shorts and the latest model trekking bike, but an old man on a rusty number with only one gear: slow.

With a sigh, Kimmie slowed down as well. The road was too narrow to pass safely.

As soon as she could, she flicked the turn signal and turned into a side street to find a faster way, but it ended up being a dead end.

She moaned quietly. Her job was fast-paced, and she was used to speed. Kimmie turned and drove back, again ending in line behind the old man and scolding herself for wasting time.

No wonder she couldn't sleep more than three or four hours a night. As soon as it was 3 a.m., Kimmie woke up. Every night. Anxious, tense, her mind racing over all the things she had to do, had done, had done wrong, had done right but could've done better, and on and on it went like a hamster on a wheel.

The old man stopped.

Kimmie stopped as well, gritting her teeth.

With some difficulty, he got off his bike, turned his head, and smiled at her. He dragged his bike to the curb and waved her on with his large, tan hand. A farmer's hand, or a carpenter's; a hand that had earned a family their living and had given food or furniture or favors to many others.

Suddenly hot with shame for her impatience, Kimmie waved back. The man stepped on the narrow sidewalk and, with an effort of his rheumatic back, heaved his bike up so Kimmie could pass more easily.

She waved again, mouthing thank you, feeling despicable.

No wonder she was divorced. They always said you had to love yourself before you could love someone else. Kimmie didn't much love herself, and sometimes, like now that she had harassed the old man off the road, she didn't even like herself.

Maybe she should call Travis. Ask him if it'd been her fault for being judgmental, for traveling too much, or working too much when she was home.

They hadn't exactly talked it out. Kimmie had returned home from a trip to Morocco one day, and her husband of only one year had been gone. Left. Left her. Left her divorce papers on the nightstand, too.

In a fit of anger, I-don't-need-anyone, and stronger-alone, Kimmie had signed and sent them to her lawyer. There'd been a prenup, so it'd been quick. No trouble. A great, no-trouble divorce. Easier than the wedding.

She bit her lip.

The GPS came back on, and a posh British voice ordered her to turn left on Herring Lane.

Kimmie almost snorted at the name but didn't.

It felt like a bit of progress.

Maybe she could be nicer again. Maybe the hard shell she'd built around herself wasn't welded in place yet. Maybe if that old man could live into his seventies and still be kind, she could do better too.

She turned into Herring Lane a little more carefully than she normally would have done.

She was going to be nice to Mom, for starters. Kimmie still didn't know why she'd suddenly fled to Bay Harbor, why Dad had forgotten her, and how Johanna fit into everything.

So many questions. And ten more minutes to Bay Harbor.

She had to find out where in town Mom was; Dad had left her to find the house, but Mom's cell had been going to voice mail all day. Maybe she'd dropped the phone in the sea. That, or she didn't want anyone to find her.

Chapter 13

Amelie ducked under the white patio umbrella that had been a gift from her son and set the platter on the table. The sun had gone down, but the velvety blue sky still reflected its glow. Later, when it was darker, they could light the citronella torches to keep mosquitoes away.

Bennett unfolded his napkin and smiled. "Oysters, Mom?"

"Yes," she declared and sat, laying her oven mitts unceremoniously beside her plate. "Roasted oysters with butter sauce. You've finished a big case; it's time to celebrate a little."

"I don't know if it's finished," he said and helped himself to a couple of steaming shells. "We have him locked up, but now comes the interviewing. I don't particularly want to know what's going on in his mind."

"I wished you'd do something happier." Amelie tried one of the oysters. It was salty and buttery and went well with the crispy Muscadet Bennett had brought from Cape Bass. She sat back and looked at the daylilies blooming across the lawn. She'd collected the bulbs from neighbors and friends over the years. Shared bulbs would have been a nice housewarming gift for Mela. But if she stayed for only a week, a bottle of the Muscadet would make more sense.

"You roasted the oysters in the oven?" Bennett nodded in appreciation. "They're great."

Amelie put her glass down. "Mela came back," she said abruptly. All evening, they'd been talking about Bennett's case, but now her news bubbled out. "Pamela, the friend I had when I was a kid—do you remember me talking about her?"

"Oh, yes. Her mother drowned, didn't she? That was why Mela had to leave Bay Harbor. She's the wife of that New Hampshire guy. You pointed her out to me once."

Bennett never forgot a thing. "That's her," Amelie confirmed. "I never saw her again in person until today. She looks great. And she's nice. I still like her a lot."

"You were tied up in her story back then," Bennett said and threw her a searching glance. "It's good she came to Bay Harbor if it gives you a chance to put the past where it belongs. Unless it digs up too many painful memories?" He stood and refilled their glasses.

"It's a little weird," Amelie admitted. "It's like I like her too much. We only spent the day together, and already I feel like she's my best friend."

"That's good, no?" He smiled and crossed his legs, wineglass in hand. "What does the psychologist say?"

"I think she's going to leave soon and probably will be too busy to return," Amelie confessed. "It seems like a blast from the past. We went to her house, which back in the day was my second home. Everything was still more or less untouched. If I'm honest, it was unsettling. I wonder how she copes."

Bennett was silent for a while. "What exactly happened to her mom?"

Amelie shrugged. "She and her brother took a sailing boat out to sea and never came back. Something happened out there. They never found the bodies or the boat."

"Did someone mess with it?" Bennett narrowed his eyes.

"I mean, nobody knows. But they said the brother built it himself, so the assumption is that it was an accident." Amelie stood, picking up the empty platter. "I made a shrimp risotto with mascarpone. It's very creamy. You'll like it."

"I'm sure I will." Bennett leaned back, his eyes on the glorious lilies. But there was a faraway quality to his gaze.

Amelie smiled. "It's too long ago, sweet son. Let that one go."

"Do you believe it was an accident?"

"Yes," she said firmly. "I do. They were brother and sister who got along very well. What else could it have been? I only remember the brother a little bit, but I know he built that boat. Grandma said he probably made a mistake, and the sail or rudder broke out at sea. Or maybe they went swimming and couldn't get back into the boat?"

"Goodness," Bennett murmured.

"It was a less safety-conscious time. Today, you can look up everything on the internet, but back then, we made it up as we went along. Truth be told, it didn't always work out." She shook her head. "Mela and I spent our days swimming in the sea and roaming the beaches and rock pools without supervision."

"Uh." Bennett moved uncomfortably. "Anything could've happened. The Cape lifeguards are always busy. You could've gotten trapped in a rip current."

"I suppose so." She smiled. It was impossible to think about those golden childhood summers and not be glad for every single day. "We survived. I mean..." Amelie caught herself. "Not all of us did. Julie didn't, and neither did her brother."

Bennett shook his head in disapproval.

Amelie understood. He'd grown up after the dawn of safety awareness. These days, everyone put on seat belts. But back when it was first made mandatory, lots of people had seen it as an outrageous invasion of privacy.

Amelie went into the kitchen where she swapped the platter for a tray loaded with plates and the bowl of steaming risotto. She'd made the savory shrimp stock herself, and it had given the rice a creamy, full flavor. The scent mingled with that of thyme roasted in olive oil and the chopped chives she'd sprinkled on top.

"Here we go," Amelie said as she lowered the tray onto the table. Bennett stood to put the plates on the table, and then he reverently picked up the bowl.

"This looks fantastic, Mom," he said, inhaling the fragrance and scooping out portions for both of them. "How long did you slave over the stove to make this?"

However difficult Bennett's cases were, he always managed to appreciate tasty food. Amelie loved that her son enjoyed the little pleasures in life and was able to take note of them.

"I didn't *slave*," she said and leaned the tray against the climbing hydrangea before she sat. "Cooking relaxes me, and I'm glad when you come so I have a reason to go all out."

"It's fantastic." Bennett closed his eyes as he chewed, his head slightly bowed. "Simply delicious."

"How aren't you married yet?" Amelie said fondly. "You're so nice."

He opened his eyes and grinned. They'd had the conversation before. "Don't know. Maybe because I barely ever spend time at home? Or the fact that I get by on ramen noodles for months? I'm much too lazy to cook shrimp risotto myself."

"You just have to make time for it," Amelie replied and tried the risotto herself. "It *is* good." The rich flavor of the shrimp and the creamy, fresh taste of the mascarpone fairly danced on the tongue.

For a while they ate quietly, enjoying the sweet summer night, the scent of the flowers, the excellent food, and cool wine. Halfway through, Bennett rose and lit the citronella torches. High above them, small bats zipped across the sky, doing their share to help.

"I have dessert," Amelie said when they'd finished and had sat a while longer.

"I'm going to get fat," Bennett replied and leaned toward her. "What is it?"

"You're not going to get fat anytime soon," Amelie said, though Bennett did have a pound or two more than he used to. But it looked good on him, though she was admittedly biased. "It's a strawberry chocolate meringue torte." She laughed at herself for having gone overboard. "Maybe Mela's return unsettled me more than I realized, and I needed the cooking to calm down."

"How did you have time for doing everything you did today?" Bennett shook his head. "You had clients too, didn't you?"

"The torte didn't take that long," Amelie deflected. "I was lucky to stumble over the recipe."

They gathered their dishes and glasses and brought them inside. Then Bennett made coffee while Amelie pulled the torte from the fridge and carefully set it on the antique milky-green glass stand she'd found at the thrift store.

"It looks beautiful, Mom," he said appreciatively. "Much too pretty to eat."

They both laughed because of course they would eat it, and Bennett carried coffee cups and plates outside.

For a moment, Amelie stepped back to admire her handiwork. She used to bake so much more—she came from a long line of pastry chefs, after all. Even if the family business had been sold, cooking and baking were in her blood.

She glanced at her son on the patio. He was sitting again in his chair, quietly looking out into the night. He looked impossibly young to her. It'd been his relentless tenacity that had catapulted him this early into the position of detective. He delivered, too. His stats were impressive and made the department look good.

She wished he could bake cakes and cookies instead of hunting criminals. Chances were, they'd both sleep easier at night.

With a sigh, she lifted the cake and carried it outside to give her child an evening of grace before he headed back out.

The torte was as delicious as it looked, and the coffee woke them up.

"How is the job search coming along?" Amelie asked carefully.

"I haven't heard anything yet, Mom. I'm sorry." Bennett set his cup down.

"Can't you stay a little longer?" Amelie asked abruptly. "Not because of me, I'm fine. But to catch a proper break."

"Summer is the busiest time for us," he said. "There are so many tourists on the Cape."

"There are plenty of officers who'd love a shot at proving themselves too," Amelie pointed out. "Let someone else have a chance to catch the bad guys. You haven't had a real vacation since you got accepted into the academy."

"Maybe you're right." Bennett tapped a crumb of meringue onto his finger and inspected it. "Maybe it is time to enjoy all this."

Amelie held her breath. "A relaxed detective is a better detective," she whispered.

He looked at her, and they both had to laugh again. "I'll see what I can do, Mom," Bennett said and stood. "Kingston might be able to stand in for me. I could use a break. Swimming in the sea sounds like a good trade for listening to a twisted mind."

"And would you want to vacation here?" Of course Bennett could just as well swim and lie on a beach towel on the Cape.

"Yes. If I stay home, I'll just end up checking in at work." Bennett stacked the cake plates. "I think I'll do the dishes and turn in. I'll make a couple of calls tomorrow morning. I don't even feel like going back."

"I'll do the dishes," Amelie said and stood as well. "I'll play some music and enjoy it, too. You go catch some sleep. I bet it's been a while."

Bennett rounded the table to kiss her cheek. "Goodnight. Thanks, Mom."

Amelie put her hand on his cheek. "You're very welcome. Goodnight, sweetheart."

He left to go upstairs. Amelie stood by herself, thinking about how life took unpredictable little turns—like Bennett vacationing in Bay Harbor—all the time. Life took big turns too, but they were rarer.

Whether Mela returning to town was a big or small turn, Amelie didn't know.

Maybe she'd find out soon. Maybe tomorrow.

Because tomorrow afternoon, she'd be back at Julie's house to watch Mela stir up the past and let it settle in new ways.

Chapter 14

I'm glad my little girl is growing up here. She'll always love the sea as much as I do.

The sun flooding in through the open balcony door woke Mela to another day. She yawned and stretched luxuriously, rolling on her side. Her gaze fell on the motel clock on her nightstand. She'd slept a whole two hours longer than usual.

Mela pushed the duvet back and sat up, ready for a day full of swimming, friends, and neighbors. She stood and, with a swing in her step, went to shower and wash her hair.

Sitting on the patio stairs the day before, she had read the first page of the recovered journal. In her long, loopy hand, Julie had written the words in the summer of 1980, on the day they'd moved into the blue house in Bay Harbor. The same year Mela had met Amelie.

Dad taught me all I need to know about beekeeping, Julie had written. *I'll get my own hives and let thousands of sisters grow up together. They'll love each other, and none of them will ever be lonely or left out. I always wonder how that would feel.*

Mela had looked at the words, perplexed. Had Julie felt lonely or left behind?

A snake had suddenly stuck out her head from the step Mela sat on. She'd jumped up and skipped away, clutching the journal so it wouldn't drop. Standing at a safe distance, she thought it was only a harmless garter snake. She wasn't sure, though, and hoped it would leave. But the snake hadn't budged.

Getting stung by a bee burned and the spot swelled, but that was it. A snakebite, on the other hand...

Mela had considered shooing the snake away with a broom but decided to wait until the next day. She was already exhausted from the wave of memories washing over her and wanted to be in a good mood for reading Julie's journal.

Mela had decided to end the day with a lobster roll from the supermarket. She ate it sitting on the beach, watching the gulls and sandpipers, even a plover or two. Plovers were her favorites; they looked like adorable wind-up toys with their little stick-legs.

Afterward, Mela had shaken the crumbs off her lap and gone back to the house to call Johanna. They needed to talk about rescheduling appointments, but the call went to voice mail. Her assistant had, however, sent a couple of emails with questions. Mela answered them and made a couple more telephone calls to find someone to fix the broken window and siding. When that was done, she had gone back to the motel and crashed, falling asleep the second she lay on the bed.

Now, Mela dried her hair with a towel, brushed it out, and dressed. Then she stepped out of her motel room. The air was already warm and smelled of freshly baked bread.

"Good morning," Peter said when she entered the reception. "How are you?" He went to fill a mug with steaming hot coffee and brought it to her, then resumed his station between computer and ledger.

"I'm very good." Mela nodded a thank you for her morning drink. "How are you, Peter?"

He leaned on the counter. "I was a bit worried you hadn't come back last night, to be honest. Sunny and I were in the backyard, eating cheese sandwiches. If we'd known you were in your room, we'd have been quieter."

"I wondered if I should find you. I guess I didn't want to bother you."

He shook his head. "No worries about bothering anyone, least of all me. We're used to checking on each other here."

"Okay. Thank you," Mela said gratefully. "It's nice to know someone cares." She sipped Peter's strong coffee, instantly feeling its effect. "I fell asleep as soon as I got to my room," she explained. "I meant to talk with my neighbor, but I was too tired. I didn't hear you two at all."

"Did Amelie wear you out?" The kind look in his eyes told her he was kidding. Amelie was clearly his friend.

She smiled. "More like cleaning house did. It's terribly dusty. And it made me emotional."

The skin between Peter's eyes crinkled into a small frown. "If there's anything I can do to help, let me know."

How could he afford to be so generous? Mela looked at him, touched. "Thank you, Peter. I will."

"Would you like breakfast?" He nodded at the door behind her.

"Yes, please," Mela said. "Did you eat already? Do you want to join me?" At home, she had breakfast alone. Rob was usually at the gym with his personal trainer in the morning.

Peter checked his watch. "I don't mind if I do."

They carried their mugs through to a table. Mela thought there was more of a spread than yesterday, including honeydew melon, flavored Greek yogurts, honey and granola, and scrambled eggs so fresh they were steaming. "This is nice," she said, helping herself to a little of each. "I can't believe the motel isn't packed to the roof with tourists."

"You should think," Peter said, pushing a bagel into the toaster. "It's close to the beach, too. I should be swimming in money."

Mela brought her plate to the table and waited for him to sit as well. "Do you have concrete plans for the motel?" she asked.

"My plan is hazy at best," Peter said. "I started out strong by furnishing a handful of rooms and getting a few cost estimates for repairs. But it turned out Dad was deep in debt, and once all that came out, everything screeched to a halt. I do what I can myself, but I don't know much about wiring and plumbing. What the place needs are tourists so I can pay the right people to fix the motel."

Mela stirred what looked like homemade roasted almond granola into a peach yogurt and tasted it. "Where did you get this from? It's so good."

"They sell it at the farmers market. You should go if you can. It's Bay Harbor's main attraction. We have people come from all over to shop locally. Well, local for us."

Mela ate another spoonful of creamy goodness. She wanted to ask about his brother. But after witnessing Peter's reaction to her mentioning Charlie, she wasn't sure she should. The brothers' relationship seemed to be a delicate topic.

"I'll tell everyone I know to come and stay at the motel," Mela said. He'd offered his help; the least she could do was offer back. "Let me know if there's anything else I can do."

He smiled. "Thank you. Too bad your husband isn't going to be governor of Maine. I'd like a connection that reaches all the way to the top."

She stirred her yogurt. "His opposition is strong."

"Do you hope he'll make it? Your husband, I mean?"

"Of course." Mela looked up, surprised. "I support his policies. If he gets elected, he will improve life for a lot of people."

Peter leaned back. “And your own life? Would that improve?”

Mela laid down her spoon. She’d lost her appetite. Of course Peter—or anyone knowing she’d arrived late in the evening, alone, without clothes or ride—knew something was amiss. “Sometimes, you have to focus on the important parts and let the rest go,” she said quietly.

The furrow between Peter’s eyes deepened. “When you say important parts, do you mean politics?”

“Yes,” Mela said. “That’s what I mean.”

Instead of telling her she should think of herself as more important, Peter nodded. “I understand,” he said gently. “Can I get you more coffee?”

“Thank you, but I better get going. I don’t have much time in Bay Harbor.”

Mela went back to her room and sat on her bed, her eyes focused on nothing. After a few minutes, she pulled out her phone and dialed Rob’s number.

To her surprise, he answered.

CHAPTER 15

Last night, Mother passed peacefully in her sleep. I hope she'll meet Grandma. When it's my turn, I want them all there, waiting for me.

"Mela. How are you?" Robert's voice was the same as always. "What happened?"

"I'm fine, Rob," she replied. "I was in the bathroom of the movie theater feeling unwell, and when I came out, everyone was gone and the doors were locked. I think I was in shock that you forgot me."

"I understand. But you know how it goes, Mela." Rob sighed. "The movie ends, people crowd around asking me a hundred questions, telling me where to go next and what to do. I'm sorry you were left behind, but I still don't understand you running away like that."

"Coming to Bay Harbor wasn't the most rational thing to do," Mela admitted. "At least Johanna wrote that it went well enough without me." She paused. "I felt lost, Rob. All I could think of was getting here to pull myself together."

"I sent Kimmie to Bay Harbor," Rob said. "She should be there already. I couldn't remember the address, so she'll be trying to find Julie's house. Maybe check the internet cafés if there are any."

Mela's heart sank a little. She'd been so looking forward to a day of fixing up the house and reading the journal at the beach. She wanted to talk more with Amelie and Peter and get to know her neighbor Sunny.

"I'll keep a lookout for Kimmie," she promised. "I have new voice messages I haven't checked yet. I'd better listen to them."

"Yes, you'd better," Rob said. His voice was even, reflecting neither anger nor empathy. "You should come back today. PR is covering for you, but they won't be able to do it much longer."

"I see."

"Also, I need you at the gala," Rob said. "I asked Kimmie to remind you. She'll drive you back."

"Okay."

"Excellent. Bye." Robert hung up.

"Bye." Mela let the phone sink. It felt like her heart slowed with disappointment in her chest. Maybe she would call the PR team and see how much effort it really took to spin her absence. Maybe it wasn't as difficult as Rob thought to cover her another day or two.

There was a knock on the door. Mela inhaled to steady herself. It was probably her eldest daughter, come to frog-march her to the gala so Rob had a wife to show off.

People were insane, Mela thought as she went to the door. Rob's politics were solid even if his marriage wasn't. What had one to do with the other? They each required a completely different skill set. But people wanted a perfect leader, not someone as messily human as themselves.

"Hello." Instead of Kimmie standing outside her door, it was the old lady from next door. She was wearing slacks and a T-shirt that had a jellyfish and the name Bay Port Aquarium on it. "I'm Sunny Gardiner, from next door."

"Hello. How can I help you?" Mela did her best to smile, but her good mood from earlier had vanished.

"I heard you coming up the stairs. Peter said you were only staying for a few days," Sunny explained. "And since you didn't stop by all day yesterday, I figured I'd better catch you while I could."

"I'm sorry." Mela exhaled through pursed lips, trying to let go of her tension. "I'm sorry," she said again, and now her smile felt genuine. "Would you like to come in?"

"Well," Sunny said, folding her hand. "To be honest, I'm spending more time in this motel than I like. I was hoping..." She inhaled as if bracing herself. "I was hoping I could come to your mom's house with you if you go back again. Maybe I can help clean or cook lunch or something."

The request was so unexpected that Mela couldn't think of anything to say. "I don't know," she said finally. "Forgive me, but—"

"I wouldn't ask usually," Sunny interrupted quickly. "It's just that Julie was my best friend. You and I only met a few times because I didn't have a car and Julie usually came to see me in Sandville. I've thought of her every single day since... Well, since we lost her. I miss her, even after all these years. I would love a chance to feel a little closer to her. Maybe it will settle some things for me. I promise I won't bother you."

"Oh. Of course, Sunny." There were other people who'd loved Julie and were still searching for closure. "I'd be happy to have your company. You can help or simply enjoy the view from the patio. It's a wonderful place to sit and look out at the sea."

Sunny's weathered face broke into a smile. "I knew why I was so fond of you back then. Julie always had to tell me what you were up to."

Mela grabbed her purse from the closet shelf and came out of the room, closing the door behind her. Her good mood was returning. How could it not, with a bubbly soul like that for her neighbor?

"Well." Mela held out her arm and smiled encouragingly. "*I* would love to hear about my mother and what *she* was up to."

Sunny hooked her hand under, and Mela supported the old lady's limp as they walked along the balcony. From the way Sunny favored one leg, Mela suspected that either her hip or knee hurt.

"She loved you. That's what she was up to." Sunny stopped to take a heavy breath. "Oh dear, the stairs.

The real reason I never leave the motel." She eyed the steps.

"Maybe if you lean on the railing and I'll take your other arm?"

"Let's give it a shot," Sunny said cheerfully. "It's my hip. I broke it jumping out of a boat, and it's never been good since. The doctor said it was busted. Not in those words, but I know what he meant."

"Have you thought about a hip replacement?" Mela grabbed Sunny tighter, taking as much weight as she could. "I have a friend who had one done. It helped very much once everything had healed."

"The surgery is expensive," Sunny said, wincing with every step. "First, I lost my hip, then my job, and then my insurance. Oh, and then my house." She chuckled as if it were funny. "Don't matter," she said consolingly as if Mela was the one who'd had the losses. "I've got Peter and my other hip. It's more than most folks have."

"You have a happy disposition," Mela remarked. "That's also more than most folks have."

They'd reached the bottom, and Sunny let out a sigh of relief. "Phew." She fanned her face with her hand. "Thank you kindly. It's nice to have firm soil under my feet."

"Why don't you stay on the ground level?" Mela asked. "So you don't have to worry about the stairs?"

Sunny shook her head. "It's either the stairs or the view of the sea. All my life I've been able to see the sea from my house. A cracked hip bone isn't going to take that from me."

"Sunny," Mela suddenly said. "I don't know if you can get in the truck. It's high."

At that moment, Peter came striding across the court of the motel, a basket of laundry in his hands and a kitchen towel slung over his shoulder. When he reached them, he set the basket on the ground and wiped his forearm over his brow. "It's hot already," he remarked. "Are you ladies off for a swim?"

"We're going to my house," Mela said. "Only..." She looked at the truck that was parked at the curb.

Peter followed her gaze. "Yeah, the beauty over there and the one standing between us don't like each other," he said. "You can drive the truck, Mela, and I'll bring Sunny in the egg. Believe it or not, it's easier for her to get into."

"Sunny?" Mela looked at the old lady.

Sunny took Peter's arm. "Sure. Beggars can't be choosers."

Mela quickly helped Peter hang up the washed sheets on the line in the backyard, and then she drove the truck to the house while he and Sunny followed behind.

She'd planned on a morning on her own, but when Mela looked at the unlikely couple in her rearview mirror, she very much liked the thought of having them in the house.

She wanted company after her call with Rob. Otherwise, she would brood over their heartless little exchange.

Keeping her eyes on the road, she speed-dialed Kimmie.

"Mom, I thought you'd never call back! Where are you? I've been driving around Bay Harbor trying to spot you on a sidewalk or in a restaurant. It's a cute place, but I'm running out of gas."

"Hi, honey," Mela said. "I'm on my way to your grandma's house at 12 Seasweet Lane. Meet me there, okay?"

"Okay." Kimmie, always short on words and time, hung up.

Mela sighed. Kimmie would want to go back right away, so Mela had to make a decision. She didn't want to leave Bay Harbor, but she couldn't just take a vacation whenever she felt like it. She had a job, and that job was supporting her husband.

She parked near the house, leaving the spot in front of the garden gate for Peter. Then she jumped out of the truck and went to help Sunny out of the egg. "Would you like to come in?" she asked Peter. "You're very welcome."

"I want a look at that siding over there." He squinted at a missing board. "I've been itching to fix it for months. I'll patch that up for you real quick."

"He's good with a hammer and nails," Sunny reported, sounding as proud as a mother.

"If you're sure, Peter," Mela said, suppressing a chuckle. "You don't have to, though. I'll have to hire someone to do the siding."

"Up to you," he said. He was still sitting on his bike, waiting for Sunny to undo the strap of the silver helmet he'd put on her head.

"Actually," Mela said, "there is one thing I'd love some help with." She smiled, feeling a little embarrassed. Here she was, a mother of three and experienced campaigner, forty-seven with the first strands of silver in her hair and afraid of a critter. "There's a snake under the porch steps. I think it's a garter snake, but...it's just so big. I'd love to know if it is harmless. I could use a second opinion."

Peter put the helmet in the egg and got off the bike. "How big?"

"Four feet, maybe? Five?"

"That's no garter snake. Maybe it's a black racer."

"Black racer?" Mela didn't like the sound of that. "Are they venomous?"

"No, but they're fast, and they like to scare people by racing toward them. Hence the name. I can try and get it out from under your stairs if it's still there. Maybe we can relocate it to a better place. They're an endangered species."

"Goodness," Mela said. "I'd like to hire you for the job, please. Name your price."

"I'm priceless," Peter quipped and followed her and Sunny to the door. "But I do what it takes to make my patrons happy."

Mela laughed. "By helping them stay in their own houses instead of the motel?" She gave the key to Peter so she could hold on to Sunny. "That would hardly be good business."

He came to stand beside her on the narrow path, meeting her gaze directly. His eyes were exceptionally light gray-blue in the bright sun, and their focus startled Mela. "Not everything I do is about business," he said. "Some people I simply want to see happy."

Before Mela could process his words, he turned away to help Sunny.

Her heart beating a little faster than before, Mela opened the door and stepped into the cool inside. She inhaled, and for a moment, the scent of her childhood enveloped her. But by the second breath it was gone already, and it smelled of the sea and the polish she'd used the day before, the old books on the shelf, the polished wood floor.

Peter and Sunny entered behind her.

"I always wondered what her house was like inside," Sunny said quietly. "Always, always wondered."

"Let me show you." Mela led her guests through to the kitchen.

Peter went to the broken window and frowned at the plastic patch, then turned and left.

The look he'd given her at the door still confused Mela.

He barely knew her. Even if they were childhood acquaintances, they also were strangers to each other.

How could he give her a look like that, full of intent and feeling?

“Peter?” Mela called out the broken window. “Couldn’t you stay awhile?”

CHAPTER 16

Mela is all I have now. I let her sweetness fill the hole in my heart the way bees fill a tree hole with honeycomb.

"I'm going to get some supplies." Peter kept striding through the front yard. "We can fix the window better than taping a piece of plastic over it. I'll just take some quick measurements. There's a tape measure in the glove compartment of the truck."

"Sunny?" Mela asked. "Take a seat, my dear. I'll be back in a moment." She followed Peter to the truck. "You don't have to fix things to stay, Peter," she said, catching him as he opened the door. "I called somebody about the window yesterday."

He leaned against the truck. "Who did you call?"

She told him the name.

"Yeah, that's what I thought," he said. "He'll come next month at the earliest. Trust me. I'll do it real quick. It'll be faster."

"Let me pay you, please? I know you offer it as a favor, but you should make it worth your time."

He crossed his arms and considered her for a long moment. That's how it seemed to Mela, anyway. He wasn't considering the price or even whether he wanted money or not. He was considering *her*.

She straightened her linen dress. "Can I ask you something that I don't know how to ask?"

He smiled. "Only because anyone would want to know what comes next. Shoot."

"You just looked at me..." She pointed at the door. "Like you wanted me to be happy for reasons that are...more."

Now his eyes smiled as well. "More? More than what?"

She tilted her head. "That's what I don't know."

He reached for her hand, taking it between his own as if it belonged to him. It felt very intimate and even more confusing than his glance earlier. Mela tried to breathe normally, as if she was used to handsome, kind men touching her casually. Of course she wasn't. Not one little bit.

"Do you remember when we were kids and you came to the motel for Charlie's tenth birthday party?" he asked, suddenly letting go again.

Mela nervously raked her mind for the memory, finding an image of herself standing on the crushed shells in the motel court in white sandals, wearing the short red dress reserved for good occasions. "Yes? Sort of."

"You brought him a helium balloon in the shape of a sea star, but when you handed it over, the string came off and it flew away."

"Oh my goodness." Now it came back to Mela. Somewhere in her mind, that balloon still existed. "I was so upset I was crying." She frowned as she again watched the sea star ascend to heaven where it had no business to be.

She'd been shocked that Charlie didn't care about losing the balloon. It'd been so hard to talk Mom into buying it for a gift, and Mela had been so proud about the way it bobbed in the air, all shiny and new and special. The other kids had run away to eat cake in the backyard and play apple bobbing. Only Peter had stayed with her.

Mela met his gaze. "You said we should go search for it."

"We went all over Bay Harbor," he confirmed. "We missed the entire party."

"And we never found the balloon." Mela laughed. "But we had fun, didn't we?" It had been the first time she'd walked around town without Mom, but she'd felt safe with Peter. "Yes, we had fun." Peter paused. "I want you to be happy, Mela." His light-blue eyes held hers as if there was more he wanted to say.

"You did make me happy," she said softly. "I think you even bought me an ice cream."

He winked at her. "Strawberry-vanilla in a cone. Do you want another one? I know a place."

She crossed her arms to keep them to herself. It felt like she was getting herself in deeper waters than she should. Her heart was beating fast, and she still wanted to throw her arms around Peter and have him hold her.

It was time to stop thinking about how good it would feel.

"You still don't have to fix my house, though," she said after a while. "You could use the time to work on the motel."

He raised his eyebrows. "I'm a grown man, Mela," he said easily. "I realize what my options are."

Mela couldn't play it cool. Giving in to the urge to touch Peter, she laid her hand on his arm. "I didn't mean to be ungracious. I genuinely appreciate your help."

He looked at her hand on his arm and then stepped away to open the door to the truck, breaking their contact. "You want to help everyone, Mela," he said, rummaging around in the glove compartment. "Maybe you should let people help you too once in a while. Not everything is a business transaction."

She flushed. "I know that," she murmured. "It's just, it doesn't feel right to make you..."

He reappeared, frowning. But when he saw her face, his forehead smoothed. He closed the door and came to her, without further ado putting an arm around her shoulder.

Just like that. As if they were old friends.

He was warm from the sun and smelled faintly of diesel engine and coffee and freshly laundered T-shirt. "Then make it feel right, Mela," he said and steered her gently back to the house. "Friends helping friends should feel right."

And suddenly, it did. Of course he was going to fix the window for her. She'd do the same for him. No questions asked, no exchange of money needed, no favor accrued to be traded in later. She opened the front door, and he let her go.

"Thanks, Peter," she said. "Thank you. For the window. But more...this." She smiled at him, a little shyer than before. The way she'd smiled back when she'd needed a knight in shining armor and he'd come to the rescue.

Peter's eyes smiled back, and then he went to inspect the damaged window.

Mela returned to the kitchen, where she found Sunny standing by the window, looking at Peter who was on the other side and staring back through the glass while slowly unraveling the measuring tape.

Sunny turned to Mela, and Peter started measuring the window frame. "Is he sweet on you?" Sunny asked, interested.

"He was just being a friend," Mela said, suppressing a laugh. "I've been gone too long."

"Because he was holding you."

"He wasn't, he was...walking me. As a friend."

"It's fine by me if he holds you because he's sweet on you. He's a good man."

"I know he's a good man."

"I can hear you, you know," Peter said through the broken window.

Mela coughed. "Let me show you the house, Sunny."

"Great. I especially want to see the garden. She was always talking about her bees."

Mela pointed the way through the porch door. "I can hardly believe it, but one of the colonies is still alive."

She helped Sunny onto the porch. The snake wasn't there, even when Mela knocked on the step.

"It's beautiful," Sunny said. "It's almost like I've been here before. Julie described it all to me."

"I wonder what she told you," Mela said. "I never got the chance to talk to her as an adult. I'd love to hear her stories."

Sunny looked at her. "I can tell you," she said. "But are you sure you want to know? You were her child, and she was careful about what she shared with you. Hearing about the other stuff might change how you feel, and Julie's not here to shape a new relationship. It'd be different."

"Things changed anyway when she was lost at sea," Mela said. "I do want to know who my mother was."

"Well, I do like telling stories." Sunny looked at the hives. "So one of them is still going?"

"At least I pretend it is." Mela went as close as she could without alarming the guards. "The stack of wood boxes is called the hive," she explained. "The bees living inside are the colony. The hive is still the one Uncle Finn built, but the colony—I can't be sure. Forty years is a long time for a colony to stick around."

"Where would the colony come from if it's not the original one?"

"Maybe it's a swarm that moved in. It could even be the offspring of the original colony." Mela chuckled. "In that case, you'd need a lawyer to decide whether it's the same colony or not."

Sunny's eyes followed the bees that landed. "That one didn't go all the way in before it took off again. Watch."

Mela did. "The foragers are busy. If something is in flower, they've got to hurry and harvest the nectar before it dries up."

"But where do they put it? I need my glasses." Sunny squinted to see better. "Don't they have to bring it inside?"

"There are other bees whose job it is to meet the forager at the entrance." Mela tried to remember what Julie had said. "Sometimes they meet just inside, sometimes outside. Those workers know exactly where the empty cells are. They take the nectar from the foragers, so the foragers can turn around and get more. Meanwhile, the hive workers bring the nectar inside and store it away."

"Very efficient," Sunny said. "I could barely get the kids to help me bring in the groceries and put them away. I think just going to the market is enough work for one person."

"It takes a lot of bees to make a spoonful of honey," Mela agreed, tucking away the information that Sunny had kids. Where were they? Why did Peter take care of Sunny instead of her children?

"But it's worth it. Honey tastes good."

"It sure does." Suddenly, Mela wanted a cup of hot peppermint tea made from crushed fresh leaves, sweetened with a teaspoon of honey. It was what she and Julie had drunk before going to bed every day during summer.

Sunny lifted her head. "I heard a knock on the door. Why doesn't Peter just come in?"

"I don't think it is Peter." Mela's heart sank a little.

Sunny patted Mela's arm. "Then you'd better check who it is."

CHAPTER 17

Kimmie pushed her aviators into her hair and stepped back. The house was cute. A small summer house, cheerful enough once an investor spruced it up. It was oceanfront property, too. That was always a big win. But there was a broken window, and the roof was wonky. So was the siding. There was too much to fix it all in a couple of days, but a real estate agent would see to it.

The door opened, and there stood Mom.

"Hi!" Kimmie said and went to hug her, genuinely glad to see her mother again. "You look different. So *flowy*. Look at you."

Mom kissed Kimmie's cheeks and stepped aside so she could enter. "I'm on vacation from business suits, I suppose."

"Yeah." Kimmie put her backpack on a rickety entrance table, getting immediate '80s vibes as if the house was part of a period movie set. "Full disclosure, Mom. Dad's sent me to discuss the vacation part." Kimmie pressed her lips together regretfully, suddenly wishing she'd have come to visit. She and mom never got enough time together.

"I'm sure," Mom said dryly.

Kimmie rubbed her arm. "So is this your mother's house? It's cute."

"Yes, this is your Grandma Julie's house. We lived here until the accident."

Kimmie leaned in to look at a crayon drawing pinned unceremoniously to the wall. It showed flowers, honeybees with an enthusiastic number of wings, and either the sea or a desert in the background. Then the penny dropped. "Oh my goodness, Mom, did you draw this?"

Mom stepped beside her to look. A smile spread over her face, and she touched a fingertip to the biggest flower. "I guess I did. I don't remember it, but I was proud of my flower drawings."

"That's pretty sweet." Kimmie would have felt the same. Kimmie would have felt the same.

Mom had been adopted at age fifteen and married at nineteen. Before that, her belongings all fit in a trash bag, which was how she carried them from foster home to foster home. The attic in the New Hampshire house had some boxes with Dad's old childhood things, but there was nothing of Mom's.

It was weird to think that at some point, Mom had sat at the kitchen table drawing while Grandma Julie moved around the kitchen, making cocoa and looking over Mom's shoulder to praise her flowers.

She let her gaze wander to the next picture. This one was a watercolor and showed the sea with two blotchy figures sitting by it, the bigger one's arm melting over the smaller figure's shoulder. "Is that you and Grandma Julie?"

"Yes." Mom turned away. "Come in, Kimmie. I have a guest who'd like to meet you."

"Oh?" Mom had only been here two days—well, two and a half. Was there someone with her? Obediently, Kimmie followed into a living room with a sofa and bookshelves and more framed kid's paintings and out through a sliding glass door to the backyard. It was stunning, but there was no time to admire the view and flowers just now.

An old woman was standing, one hip higher than the other, in front of a beehive. When she heard them coming, she turned around.

"Sunny, this is my daughter," Mela introduced her. "Kimmie, this is an old friend of my mother's."

"Hello, Julie's grandchild," the old lady said. "I'm Sunny."

"I'm Kimmie," Kimmie said and held out her hand. "Nice to meet you."

It was strange to hear herself called Julie's grandchild. As if she was being handed a secret identity.

She already had a full set of grandparents—Dad's parents, who lived close to the family home in an exclusive New Hampshire retirement community, and Mom's adoptive parents, Angela and Harry, who'd moved to Vermont after they'd retired. When Kimmie had been little, they'd visited twice a year, but now it was usually just a zoom call to say hi and bye.

"Your mom knows a lot about bees," Sunny said and pointed at the old beehives.

"Mom, I had no idea." Kimmie moved a little closer to the house. She couldn't tell a honeybee from a bumblebee and didn't care to learn the difference. They all stung as far as she knew.

"You're all right, Kimmie," Mom said calmly. As usual, nothing escaped her blue eyes.

Kimmie shivered. "I don't like getting stung."

"You drive into war zones and do who-knows-what, sweetheart," Mom said and smiled. "You can definitely handle a bee sting."

"Maybe I can. But I don't want to."

"Let me show you two the house," Mom said. She went to Sunny and took her arm, helping the old lady hobble inside. Kimmie followed slowly, turning for another look at the beach. It was right down there. A quick walk through the field behind the flower beds, and you'd hit the sand.

It'd be pretty fun to grow up here.

Kimmie pictured herself at six or seven, getting up on a bright summer morning and running down the path to the beach with her siblings before breakfast.

She felt a pang of regret.

They'd spent the few family vacations they'd taken over the years in Aruba, where Dad's parents owned a hotel apartment. Aruba was great, but this was wilder and more unfettered than the hotel environment. Dinner and a show had been fun when they'd been kids, but this was the sort of place where you'd eat a bowl of spaghetti in your swimsuit before running off to catch fireflies and dip into the sea for a quick good-night-swim. Even Sis and Morris would've liked that.

"Kimmie, do you want to join us?" her mom called from the house.

"Sure." Kimmie stepped into the cool inside. Now she was curious and wanted to see everything. The kitchen table where Mom had drawn her picture and eaten the mussels Grandma Julie had collected, Mom's room, Julie's room. Kimmie even wanted to see the attic, if there was one.

She helped Mom bring Sunny upstairs, and the old lady rewarded her with a pat on the cheek that made Kimmie smile. Maybe she was a little bit nice to people after all.

Mom opened a door. "This was Julie's room."

Kimmie stepped inside, and Sunny and Mom followed. They stood as if in a museum, silent, pensive, taking it in. Wordlessly, Mom hooked her arm under Kimmie's, and Kimmie put her free hand on Mom's.

"I crocheted this afghan for her," Sunny suddenly said. She went to the bed and picked up a folded blanket, spreading it out. "It was for her birthday."

Kimmie felt her heart warm another degree toward the old lady. Maybe she needed more people in her life who patted cheeks and made their friends blankets.

"She used it all the time," Mom said. Sunny handed her the afghan, and Mom took it, lifting it to her face and pressing her cheek into it.

Kimmie didn't often remember that Mom had a small child inside of her just like every other person. But here, Mom's childhood had been frozen into place, and it felt sweet and messy at the same time.

"I picked out the sheets with her too," Sunny said quietly.

"Did you?" Mom went to Sunny and put a hand around her shoulder. "It's a strange feeling, isn't it?"

Kimmie looked at the two hugging, wishing she, too, could have met her grandmother. As far as she knew, neither Grandma Julie nor her brother had ever been found. The coast guards had told Mom that the currents would have washed the ship out to sea, not back to the coast.

Kimmie went to the armoire and opened it. "Mom, look." She pulled one of the long dresses out. It had an off-shoulder white ruffle top, an elastic waist, and an ankle-length skirt. Easy breezy vintage, perfect for the beach and begging to be paired with Farrah Fawcett hair.

"You're wearing a modern version of it," Kimmie said suddenly. "The color is almost the same." Mom's dress was similar, only straight-cut and with spaghetti straps instead of an elastic ruffle across the shoulders.

Mom came to stand by her and touched the fabric. "I remember that dress."

Sunny suddenly turned and limped out of the room. Kimmie locked eyes with Mom. "Too much?" Kimmie asked quietly, hanging the dress back and closing the closet.

"I think so. Go have a look at the other rooms, honey. I'll take Sunny downstairs."

Mom went after the old lady, and Kimmie continued exploring.

Mom's old room had a tiny bed and a shelf for toys, a low bookshelf, desk and chair, and, for some reason, a freestanding coat rack in the corner by the door. Pinned to the walls were posters of horses looking over fences. The wall by the bed was covered with stickers, some of them intact, others peeling at the corners. And like in Julie's room, a big window framed the sea.

There were two more unfurnished bedrooms upstairs, both looking out on the street, and a large bathroom with a tiled floor and a clawfoot tub.

Kimmie picked a teddy bear from Mom's bed; she'd ask if she could keep it. She hadn't kept any of her own stuffed toys, but the fat little bear touched her heart. Had the people who took Mom to her foster family let her take some toys?

Kimmie went downstairs and sat the teddy on the sofa to ask for permission later. Then she went to join Mom and Sunny in the kitchen.

"I'd like to clean this kitchen," Sunny said when she entered. "It's been ages since I've done that." She sighed. "But if you'd like some time alone, say the word. I'm sure Peter can pick me up."

"I like having you here," Mom said. "It makes it easier."

"Easier?" Kimmie asked before thinking. "Is it hard to be here, Mom?"

Mom turned to her. "There's a lot that's coming back to me. And some I never knew."

This Mela was new to her—not the professional, efficient woman Kimmie knew, but someone vulnerable trying to find her way. "Can I do anything to help?" Kimmie asked.

"Could you help Sunny find what she needs? I'd like to sit outside for a moment. By myself."

Mom didn't sit by herself, so that was even more unsettling. "Sure." Kimmie turned to Sunny and smiled tentatively. "What would you like to do?"

"Clean the sink. I swear I saw an eye look out at me from the drain."

"Eww." Kimmie had to laugh. "Let's see what we can find in the cabinets. Sponges and scrubbing brushes would be good, and some dish soap."

Kimmie bent to check the space below the sink, rifling through an array of bottles. Dust had collected on them, but a couple of them hadn't even been opened yet. "Do you prefer Sunlight, Joy, or Dawn?" she asked over her shoulder.

Sunny chuckled. "Sunlight with the lemons, child."

Kimmie grabbed the bottle and stood.

Maybe Dad should be the one to talk Mom into coming home. Because as far as Kimmie saw it, success was not guaranteed.

CHAPTER 18

Little Charlie kissed Amelie today, and it made her cry. Are boys born behaving like that? I wanted to ask his mom, though of course I didn't. We laughed it off, but I took the girls home soon after.

Mela put down the journal and stretched. She'd been reading a few more of Julie's entries, savoring each one. Every day had a little note about Mela too, the sand dollar she found, the dish she liked, the friend she visited. Amelie's name showed up a few times, and Sunny was mentioned gratefully.

When it came to Finn, the notes were short and clipped. More jot-downs of reminders than thoughts, which was a little curious. Maybe it was like that with brothers.

The sliding door hummed open, and Sunny appeared, wiping her hands on a kitchen towel. "The kitchen is clean enough to think about cooking lunch, but I need to rest first. Can I join you for a bit?"

"Please." Now that she'd read how much their friendship had meant to Julie, it was like making the elderly woman's acquaintance all over again. She stood to help Sunny down the stairs.

"Sit here." Mela nodded at the vacated step. It was high enough for Sunny to sit on without too much pain.

"No snakes?"

"I promise there are no snakes. Peter checked."

He'd come back shortly after Mela had started reading, interrupting her only long enough to shine a flashlight under the step and make sure there were no endangered black racers. Mela had been relieved her nice seat wasn't a snake den. Peter had seemed disappointed, murmuring to himself as he went to fix the window.

"Sunny," she said suddenly. "Do you know who my father is?"

"No, honey. Julie never talked about it."

"Would you tell me if you knew?"

"Yes." Sunny nodded. "I would. I honestly don't know."

"Well, I still have half a journal left," Mela said. "I'm tempted to flip through it, but there are so few pages I'm holding myself back. I want to take my time and enjoy every entry. Maybe my answers are still waiting for me."

"I hope you'll find them," Sunny said. "Julie liked to chat, but some things she didn't talk about."

"Like who my dad was."

"I also know next to nothing about your grandmother, Constance. If Julie mentioned her family at all, she talked about you."

"I'm glad she at least had Uncle Finn," Mela said. "And you. She wrote about how much she enjoyed your company."

"Same here." Sunny sighed. "We were dialed into the same wavelength or something."

"Where's Kimmie?" Mela asked.

"She left to get coffee. I figured she wants you to go back to New Hampshire," Sunny said. "She's not dressed for summer vacation at the coast, is she? Are you going to go with her?"

"I should. It's not the best time for a vacation."

"Ah, the story of life," Sunny said and turned her face back into the sun. "What would you do if you stayed?"

Mela let her gaze wander. "I want to clean out the hive boxes and put new colonies into them."

She turned and saw Sunny blink at her.

"Do you know how to do that?"

"Beekeeping?" Mela laughed. "It's in my blood, though I'm sure there'd be trial and error. I helped Mom as much as I could, which meant standing around in a veil, handing her things, and watching closely. I had my very own hive tool. Maybe it's still around somewhere."

"You can find it," Sunny encouraged her. "I bet that little shed by the apple trees over there is where she kept the bee stuff."

"You're right. We kept the beekeeping equipment in the shed. I'll have to find the key for the padlock. Give me a minute."

Mela had barely made it inside, rummaging through the odds-and-ends kitchen drawer, when there was a knock on the door. "Come on in," she called. "It's open."

The door scraped open and shut again. "Hi! It's me, Amelie."

Mela turned in time to see her friend enter the kitchen. "Good to see you, Amelie!"

"You too," Amelie said and returned the smile. "I'd have come sooner, but one of my clients had a bit of a breakdown right at the end of the session, and I couldn't send them out the door crying. I never can."

"I'm glad you're here now," Mela said. "I was afraid I'd been a bit much yesterday after all."

"Not a chance," Amelie said. "I brought my son. Is that okay?"

"It is! I'd love to meet him. My daughter came for a surprise visit too. She went out to get coffee, but she should be back any moment."

"Oh good." Amelie went to look out the kitchen window, then waved Mela to join her.

Mela had finally found the key to the bee shed. It had a curly piece of gift ribbon on it. She finagled it out from under a wire brush and a spilled box of toothpicks. "What is it?"

"Is that lovely lady in black your daughter? Look."

Mela went to the window and looked out. On the curb in front of the house stood Kimmie, a carton tray of paper coffee cups in her hands. She was talking animatedly to a handsome young man who had Amelie's gorgeous almond eyes.

"Oh," she said. "Look at that."

They watched a little longer. "Is she available?" Amelie asked interestedly.

"She's freshly divorced," Mela said. "Whatever emotional state that translates to."

"Why? Was it his fault? Tell me it was his fault."

Bennett was laughing at something, and Kimmie laughed, too.

"You'd have to ask her." Kimmie had presented the divorce as a done deal to Mela. There'd been no tears, no explanations, and a crystal clear prenup. But the next time she'd met her eldest, Mela had gotten the impression things weren't quite as crystal clear when it came to Kimmie's feelings. "I only know they were both terribly busy. She's traveling a lot."

"Hmm." Amelie weaved her head. "Bennett can lose a few weeks over a case himself. I don't know. It could be a perfect match."

Mela had to swallow a chuckle. "We can always just get them married and see how it works out," she said, keeping her voice level. "Maybe we get lucky."

"Right? Oh, they're coming. Act normal." Amelie whisked away from the window, smacking into Mela, who was doing the same. Their shoulders met with a soft thud.

"Ouch!" Mela started laughing.

They were still giggling when Kimmie and Bennett came into the kitchen.

Kimmie put her coffee tray on the table. "Anything we should know about?"

Mela straightened and cleared her throat. "Kimmie, this is my friend Amelie," she said.

"Nice to meet you, Amelie," Kimmie said politely.

"Bennett, this is my friend Pamela." Amelie was still grinning, and Mela saw Bennett narrow his handsome brown eyes.

"Ah," he said and held out his hand. "Very nice to meet you, Pamela. I've heard a lot about you, and only the very best."

"It's so nice to meet you," Mela said and shook. "Call me Mela, if you don't mind. Only my enemies call me Pamela."

"Come now, Mom," Kimmie said. "Lots of people call you Pamela."

Mela smiled at Bennett. "Still," she said. "Call me Mela. I like it better."

"I will," he promised.

Kimmie frowned at her tray. "I brought coffee, but now it seems there are too few drinks."

"Luckily, I brought coffee too," Peter said from the door.

"Peter! Everyone, this is Peter. He's the brother of my..." Mela caught herself. Peter was more to her than a brother. "He's my childhood friend."

"Hi." Peter came inside and put another loaded carton tray beside Kimmie's. "I also bring donuts. There's a little store in town where you can custom order them. They're freshly baked, and I thought it was a good reason to run a little late."

"Thank you," Mela said. She wanted to say more to him but couldn't think of anything. She was still thinking of the way he'd looked at her earlier and the way his arm had felt on her shoulders.

"Mom? Should I?" Bennett pointed at a car parked outside, and Amelie nodded.

"Did you all have lunch?"

"No," Mela said. "But Sunny wanted to cook something."

"I didn't get around to it. We had to clean first," Sunny called. "Peter, help me with these stairs!"

"Yes, ma'am." Peter put down his box of donuts and left the kitchen.

Mela's stomach suddenly grumbled. "Now that you've mentioned lunch, I'm suddenly hungry."

Sunny came into the kitchen, leaning on Peter's arm, and sank onto a kitchen chair. "You forgot about me, Mela," she said, trying to catch her breath.

"Not at all," Mela said and held up the bee shed key. "It's just that people keep coming in."

"Do you mind?" Kimmie asked, looking surprised.

"I love it!" Mela hooked her arm under Amelie's and pulled her close. "It's the best."

"Bennett, sweetheart, would you mind getting the food from the car?" Amelie asked, patting Mela's hand on her arm.

"I...don't, Mother." Bennett threw her a look as if he minded being called sweetheart in front of a crowd.

Peter grinned.

"I'll help you." Kimmie followed Bennett outside.

Amelie nudged Mela, and they went to the window to watch.

CHAPTER 19

Today, I started writing Mother a letter before I remembered she is gone. I have so many questions without answers.

The kids came back into the kitchen, each lugging an insulated bag.

"I woke up too early and whiled away the time cooking," Amelie said, unzipping the bags and putting large lidded foil trays on the table.

"What is it?" Sunny asked, pulling one close.

"Pomegranate-glazed chicken," Amelie popped off a lid. The savory-sweet scent of fruit, molasses, and butter-roasted pine nuts filled the kitchen. Everyone took a deep breath.

"With a side of coconut rice." Amelie opened another tray. "I have no idea whether they go together, but I bought too many bags of coconut flakes and have to use them up."

"It sounds like a good combination to me," Peter said. "The coffee will stay hot for a while, or we can put it in the freezer and drink it cold. Might be better in this weather anyway."

Kimmie looked at the cups as if she wanted hers badly, but then she nodded. "Let's ice them." She looked for approval and slid the trays into the empty freezer. When she was done, she started to open cabinets. "Where are the plates, Mom?"

Mela's heart widened. She knew where the plates should be; in the same place she and Julie had stacked them after their last dinner together. Now her daughter would take them out for the first time since then. It was almost like Kimmie joining her and Julie in the mundane task of setting a table.

"Mom?"

"Plates are in the cabinet to your left," Mela said. "Silverware is in the drawer beside the stove."

"Can we eat outside?" Peter asked. "The view from the yard is too beautiful to miss."

"What about the bees?" Kimmie asked.

"Just don't swallow one, hon," Sunny said. "I'll take myself outside, everyone. At least you don't have to carry me."

"You can also take the napkins if you like," Mela said and handed Sunny a kitchen paper roll that was fresh from the '80s . It'd be good for Sunny to feel like she was pitching in. Mela would look into crutches, though she suspected Sunny had one and didn't use it. Mela would also look into hip replacements. There had to be a way of giving Sunny back her mobility.

Bennett and Peter carried the small kitchen table and the chairs outside, and Amelie and Mela brought the food and silverware. Mela came back and filled glasses with water, and Kimmie helped carry them outside.

Bennett and Kimmie filled their plates and sat on the step, their knees almost touching. The rest of them sat at the table.

Peter jumped again and went inside, then returned with a potted lavender that had been trained into a small tree. He handed it to Mela. "This one's for you," he said. "It's only from the hardware store, but bees like lavender, don't they?"

She took the fragrant plant and inhaled the scent. "Yes, and so do I. Thank you very much."

"A little housewarming gift," he said.

Mela hadn't forgotten Peter's words that he wanted her to be happy. Busily, she turned around, fussing to find a good spot for her tree.

When she'd recovered, they sat and started eating. The chicken was juicy from a yogurt marinade and crispy with a pomegranate-molasses crust. Amelie had baked it to perfection.

They took their time with the meal. When they were done, the sun had passed the highest point in the azure sky. Peter and Bennett cleared the table and brought out the donuts and iced coffees, and they took even longer to finish those.

Mela leaned back, a tiny donut with strawberry icing in one hand and a creamy coffee in the other.

She'd given dozens of dinners and brunches and lunches, but this was one of the best. She loved everything about it, down to the green '70s vine pattern on Julie's cheap melamine plates. But the real secret was of course the company, their easy chatter and laughter. Even Kimmie seemed to be having a wonderful time.

It was good to see. She'd become too joyless and harried, and Mela hadn't seen her laugh properly since the divorce. No matter what Mela and Amelie might say for a joke, Kimmie wasn't over her ex. It was good to see her smile and even flirt with Bennett.

Maybe Mela could turn Kimmie's intention of bringing her back around and talk her daughter into staying in Bay Harbor instead?

Amelie touched her arm. "Are you okay?"

"I'm great." If it hadn't been for Rob and the world of politics, Mela would've felt perfect. She popped the donut into her mouth. It was soft and chewy, filled with a fresh strawberry cream that was the flawless ending to the meal.

"Let's go swimming," she said as soon as she could.

"Now? Is that a joke?"

"Carpe diem," Mela declared. "Did you bring your suits?"

"Yeah, but..."

"Well then—first one in the water wins." She grinned a challenge at her friend.

Amelie looked back almost with shock. "We just—"

Instead of waiting, Mela stood and made a beeline for the bedroom; behind her, Amelie's chair scraped over the patio stone.

Upstairs, Mela shook the black suit from the bag and snipped the tags, then changed into it. She decided against putting on a coverup in case Amelie didn't bring one and would feel self-conscious about it. Then she slipped into the gas station flip-flops and made her way back downstairs and out the glass door.

"I'm coming!" Amelie was right behind her.

Mela turned and laughed. Not about the way her best friend looked in her joyfully cherry-red suit. She laughed out of delight because they got to do this again—swim together in the sea on a beautiful summer day in Maine. Instead of racing ahead, she held out a hand. "You look stunning, Amelie."

"I agree," Peter said. He'd put his feet up on an empty chair and was looking at them with a smile. Even Bennett and Kimmie nodded their approval, and Sunny clapped her hands.

"Well done, girls," she said. "I would join you if I could; I don't care how I look in a suit."

Amelie looked at Mela, on her face an expression of amused disbelief about the situation. Mela thought it probably matched her own. Then Amelie grabbed Mela's hand. Swinging hands as if they were ten years old again they walked down to the sea.

"I'm coming too!" Kimmie called out after them, and then there was a general scraping of chairs interrupted by chatting and laughing and Bennett saying, "Shouldn't we wait? We just ate lunch."

They'd reached the beach. "I waited long enough," Mela said. She pulled her hair back and kicked off her sandals.

The water lay like a shimmering jewel in front of them, the blue waves waiting to embrace them. Mela dipped her toe in. "It's *cold*!" she screamed.

Amelie laughed and started running into the water, pulling Mela with her.

There was none of the usual dignified wetting of legs and trunk, gingerly spreading of hands on the water or undecided squinting. There was only full-on joy about life and friends and summer at the sea.

They let themselves fall forward in a dance they'd memorized as kids, bellies and breasts breaking the surface first, flailing arms and legs last.

Mela's face was underwater, her eyes wide open. She kicked as hard as she could to get farther into the deep, and then she dove and twisted and saw the sun shining through the waves above, the rays breaking on the blue surface and dancing down, down, down.

It was beautiful.

This was what her mother had seen.

Mela let herself sink lower, below the moving waves, below the last forty years, and into the depth she'd known as a child.

A shadow shot across her, and a hand grabbed her wrist, pulling her up, higher and higher and back to the light until she broke the surface.

CHAPTER 20

What would I do without Sunny? She is the one I run to. Today she said she'll always be there for me, and I said the same to her.

Peter was standing beside her in the water that reached to the top of his chest, fully dressed.

Mela gasped for breath, finding the sandy bottom under her feet. She slicked her wet hair back to see.

"Mom?" Kimmie screamed from the beach.

"Current," was all Peter managed to get out. "I thought you got caught."

Mela wiped the water off her face. "I'm fine. There's no current. I was having a blue moment."

"Yeah," Peter said. "Exactly." He closed his eyes and opened them again slowly.

"I'm sorry. I didn't mean to scare—"

He threw himself forward into the water, lunging for her. Before Mela could react, Peter threw her over his shoulder, holding her tight so she couldn't wiggle her way out of his arms. She squealed and heard Amelie laugh. Again, Kimmie screamed something.

"Let me down!" Mela yelled, kicking up water with her feet. She was laughing so hard she could barely get the words out.

"I'm saving you whether you want it or not," Peter growled. He turned and strode toward the beach. A few steps anyway, until the water reached his belly, then he let her go. Amelie swam up to them, gasping for air between laughs.

Mela grinned at her and tried to punch Peter's arm but lost her balance and toppled backward. He caught her and set her back on her feet, shaking his head, eyes crinkling. "Looks like you need me!"

Kimmie screamed again, and Mela turned to wave.

There, behind her daughter, stood Robert.

He was barefoot, the hem of his slacks folded to expose his ankles. His face was carefully neutral.

"Oh." Again, Mela pushed her hair back so she could see. The salt water was already drying on her shoulders. "I better go and say hi to my husband."

Peter turned to look. "He looks exactly like on TV," he said.

Amelie, too, stopped laughing.

Together, they waded out of the water.

"Rob," Mela said when she was close enough to be heard. "What are you doing here?"

Sunny held out a towel, and Mela gratefully took it, wrapping it around herself. Bennett had more towels for his mother and Peter.

Peter dabbed his face and arms dry. His jeans and blue T-shirt were soaked and sticking to his chest.

Unfortunately, he had a clearly outlined six-pack that was nothing short of admirable. "I thought she'd gone under," he said and held out his hand. "No harm meant."

"Of course not," Rob said and smiled his diplomatic smile as he shook Peter's hand. "Thank you for keeping an eye out for Pamela." He wiped his hand on his slacks, and then he lifted his elbow and looked at her.

Mela recognized the signal. She stepped into her flip-flops and obediently took her husband's arm.

"Let's go talk for a minute, Pamela." Rob looked around the loose circle of friends. "If you'll excuse us. Kimmie—if you don't mind, we'll see you at the house in five."

Kimmie's eyes went to Mela. Mela nodded, and her daughter pressed her lips together in something like disappointment. "Sure, Dad."

"Peter, it's my turn to get my feet wet," Sunny said.

Everybody was polite enough to take the cue, turning away, resuming some sort of conversation.

Robert started walking, taking Mela with him. She looked back over her shoulder, catching Amelie's eye. Amelie gave a small wave with her hand, and again, Mela nodded; she was okay.

"You want to talk?" she asked. Usually, she was in charge of starting relationship talks.

"Yes," he said dryly. "That's why I canceled my afternoon appointments and flew out here. I have to be back tonight, and I'd like it if you came back with me."

Mela's thoughts raced back to her schedule as she followed him through the field. "The gala ball isn't until tomorrow night, Robert," she said. "I still have today."

They'd reached the stone wall to the backyard. Robert let her go, waiting until she passed ahead of him through the little wooden gate.

Mela sat on her chair. The lunch plates were still on the table. Seeing it with Rob's eyes, it looked like a mess. She pried a coffee from a tray and took a sip to wash the salt from her mouth.

"What is this nonsense, Mela?" Rob sat in the chair beside her. "I understand you want a vacation." He let his gaze wander across the neglected yard, the overgrown flower beds. "Or maybe I don't. Anyway. It's fine if you want to fix Julie's house, but..." He lifted his hands and let them drop again. "*Now* is not the time, Mela. Now is not the time to run off like a teenager."

"I'm not," Mela said firmly, "a teenager. You left me in the theater, Rob. You only noticed I was gone when... Who knows? When Johanna pointed it out, probably."

He shook his head once. "Now is not the time to be overly sensitive either, Pamela."

"I'm not—" Mela stopped and reigned her voice back in. "I'm not *overly* sensitive, Rob. I'm sensitive. It's a good thing. I like being sensitive. It's better than being callous."

He looked at her, a frown cracking the space between his eyebrows. "After the election, you can do as you like. For now, I need you to play your part."

"I know." Mela put her elbows on the table and covered her eyes with her hands. She wanted it to be different. She wanted to stay here. She wanted to enjoy her life while she could. She wanted to show life at the sea to her daughter. She wanted to share her life with her friend Amelie, she wanted to make sure Sunny was taken care of, she wanted to discover what she didn't remember. She wanted to get to know Peter.

There was so much she wanted to do in Bay Harbor.

"The thing is, Rob." She uncovered her face and looked at her husband. "As far as our life goes, playing a part is all I'm doing anymore."

"We all do, and now is not the time to stop." He opened his hands as if he was stating the obvious.

The sun was hot on Mela's naked shoulders, and she crossed her arms and covered them with her hands. "All this time, I thought I was your sidekick, Rob," she said, sorting through her thoughts as she talked. "Mostly invisible, but helpful. Best supporting actor, you know?"

"No. I have no idea what you're talking about."

"Now I think I wasn't even that. Maybe you wouldn't have come as far without me as you have, but what is the difference worth?"

A sour expression came over his face. "What is it worth? You know exactly what it's worth. You know the policies; you know how they would help the people. You don't make sense."

"I don't want to always make sense," she said. "I want to enjoy my life. Who knows how much time I have left?" Suddenly, panic settled over her. How much time *did* she have left? How could she spend any more time at luncheons and dinners, lectures and speeches and balls, a smiling mask fixed on her face?

But if that was her no... What was her yes?

This? The sun, the beach, her mother's little house, a good friend or two?

If she knew she'd have to leave as unexpectedly as her mother, would she want this to be her yes?

"You're burning up," Robert said and pointed at her shoulder. "Come on, Mela, don't be ridiculous. You're too old for this."

"All right," Mela said quietly. "I'll come back with you. Just give me half an hour to pack and say bye to everyone."

CHAPTER 21

I stayed with Sunny until the kids came home. We told them it was a bee sting. Sunny swears she's done, but I'm not so sure she can leave him.

"Mela? Two minutes until we should go downstairs," Johanna said behind her. She was folding clothes into neat little piles on the bed. Mela, fully gowned in a designer affair and with rented jewels glistening on her neck and wrists, was sitting at her desk.

She closed the journal and put it into the drawer, feeling sick. Sunny had been in a troubled marriage, yet she seemed so determined to be happy. But maybe adversity had made her so strong.

Mela rose. "I'm coming."

Her hair was pinned at the nape of her neck. Already the weight made her scalp hurt. In Bay Harbor, it'd been flying in her eyes, but nothing had hurt.

"Here." Johanna brought the high heels and set them on the floor. She, too, was gowned and braided, but less elaborately.

"Thank you." Mela lifted her rustling skirt and stepped into the shoes. Johanna had stored her pink flip-flops in the basement somewhere. Maybe she'd even thrown them away.

Mela glanced out of the window. It was evening, hot and humid, with a hazy sun just settling on the treetops. The forest was black already, stoic and still.

She liked the forest. It was nice to take walks in the shade, and the fall colors were spectacular. But Mela loved the sea.

"Are you okay?" Johanna asked.

"Yes. I'm fine. How are you?"

Johanna smiled. "I'm hanging in there."

Mela was about to ask if they should go when Johanna cleared her throat. "Ma'am?"

Johanna didn't often call her ma'am. She usually called her Mela.

"Yes?"

"I just wanted to say..." Johanna took a deep breath and exhaled. "I just wanted to say I'm very glad you're back."

"Oh." Mela was touched. "I'm sorry I left you hanging, Johanna. Everyone was so busy I didn't think my absence mattered very much."

Johanna lowered her gaze. "It took me longer to notice than it should have," she admitted. "I feel terrible about it. My priority should have been to make sure you were taken care of. Um..."

Mela waited for a moment, but it seemed as if Johanna was done talking after all. "You had too much on your list that day. No worries," Mela said. She wanted to add that her husband should've been the one to notice, but that would've been unprofessional, petty, and possibly false. Rob wasn't in charge of tracking everyone's schedules. Mela swallowed the words back down. Instead, she went to Johanna and pulled her into a quick hug.

"Should we go?" she asked. "I saw the limo pull into the driveway."

"Yes." Johanna's face flushed pink. She grabbed the purses and handed Mela a tiny mother-of-pearl clutch. "It looks like a treasure from the sea. Just beautiful." Johanna's own clutch was made of simple black satin. She slipped her cell phone into it. "Do you have your phone too, Mela?"

"I think so," Mela said. "It's somewhere in my dress." The mother-of-pearl clutch was pretty but too small for the phone. "Let's do this," she said and left the bedroom. Lifting layers of taffeta and silk like a matron of the past, she did her best not to trip on the staircase.

Johanna was close behind her.

Mela thought it was nice her assistant had apologized. But there'd been that unfinished feel to her words. Maybe Johanna had meant to tell her something more. Maybe something entirely different. Maybe she still would.

Rob came fully tuxedoed out of the study, a posse of bodyguards around him. There'd been some threats made, and his security had been upgraded. He nodded at the women, his eyes assessing first Mela's looks, then Johanna's. Wordlessly, he led the way outside.

"Huh," Mela said when the humid, hot forest air hit her. "I wish there was a breeze."

"Be glad there isn't," Johanna murmured behind her. "It would mess up your hair. I don't think I could get Francesca back in time to pin it again. She's got another client due at the gala."

They rustled and poofed their way into their cars.

Robert, sitting opposite them in the limousine beside his favorite guard, was on his cell phone for the entire drive.

They'd barely spoken to each other since Mela had come back. He might have been angry, but more likely he was distracted by his job. Even for someone who enjoyed being in the public eye, the job was too much. There'd been some negotiations that had fallen through. The press still circled like vultures, determined to tear up every last bit of the carcass.

She glanced at his phone and saw him flipping through articles his team had linked for him. "It'll be all right," Mela said. "It'll work out. We can pivot."

He looked at her in mild surprise. "Even if we don't, it doesn't matter. This one's not going to affect the ratings."

She blinked. Ratings mattered, but the policy had addressed community housing. "You can't drop it," she said. "It's necessary."

He set his phone to silent and slipped it into his pocket. "I decide what's necessary," he said quietly.

"You be the sidekick. That's what you said you wanted to be, wasn't it? A hand in the game without too much responsibility."

Mela glanced at Johanna, who was sitting beside her. The young woman was looking down at her lap. "Josh and Benjamin are working on the housing project, ma'am," she whispered.

The two young men were eager, and they got results.

Mela exhaled. "I take responsibility for plenty of things, Rob," she replied. "I raised your children and stood by your side, working fourteen-hour days for decades so you could be where you are today."

He frowned but didn't reply.

Mela turned away. She felt sick to her stomach. Her job was different from her husband's. For him to gloss over everything she contributed was unfair. More, it was harsh.

The ball was a success. There were many courses at the dinner, donations were made, beautiful C-list celebrities cracked jokes on stage, and Rob shook eager hands.

He smiled at Mela when he finally led her to the dance floor to swelling applause. "I'm sorry, Mela," he whispered. "It's been a crazy campaign. I didn't mean to forget you at the ballet."

She smiled back because there was nothing else to do when hundreds of eyes were watching. When had he gone to the ballet? She'd not been in years and couldn't remember seeing it on the schedule.

Once back home, she kicked off the heels in the foyer and went upstairs. Rob had gone straight from the resort to the airport.

A little later, she heard Johanna knock and enter. "Mela?"

Mela stood. "Help me out of this thing," she said and lifted her arms so Johanna could undo the tiny hidden buttons Mela couldn't reach. "I just want to go to bed."

"You didn't have a good time?"

"Did you?"

"It was a nice ball. The food was good."

The buttons were undone, and the gown rustled to the floor like a pile of old leaves.

"Thank you." Mela stepped out of it in her silk slip. "I've got it from here." Johanna was already dressed in a soft crop-top sweat suit. "Go ahead and get yourself into bed." Mela went to fetch her robe.

Instead of going to the guestroom Johanna used when she stayed over, she picked up the gown.

Mela turned. She wanted to be alone. She wanted to go to bed and think about the blue house on Seasweet and the people she'd met in Bay Harbor. "I can hang up the gown," she said. "It's late, Johanna. You've done enough today."

She pulled a pin from her hair, sighing as the coil loosened and fell. She caught her image in the mirror as she went to the dresser to put it in the china bowl she kept for pins. Her reflection showed how she felt—exhausted.

Johanna was busying herself hanging the gown.

For a moment, Mela watched her in the mirror. It was going on three in the morning.

When Johanna really couldn't find another ruffle to pat back in place and looked up, their eyes met in the glass. "Is there something you'd like to talk about?" Mela asked softly.

"Was it nice in Bay Harbor?"

Mela pulled another pin from the twist. "It was very nice."

"You have a house there?"

"My mother's house. It's fairly small. Nothing like this." Mela pulled out the last pin and turned. "Out with it, Johanna. It's getting late."

"Just...if you go back, ma'am, would you mind taking me?"

"Take you? To Bay Harbor?"

"Yes. If you can." Johanna smiled, looking embarrassed. "It wasn't much fun here without you, and I've always dreamed of living at the sea. I feel bad for asking because I am grateful for this job. I can stay here and take care of things if you need me to. Just..." She inhaled. "I thought I'd ask if next time, I can come. Since I'm your assistant, I enjoy working with you more than...than..." She stopped, her cheeks flushing pink.

Mela tilted her head. "Did something happen, Jo?"

Johanna looked at her hands. "No, ma'am."

There was only one other person Johanna worked for. "Did Rob try anything?" Mela shocked herself, saying the words. Rob had always been faithful. At least as far as she knew.

A frown wrinkled Johanna's brow. "I'm sure it was the stress," she whispered. "It wasn't—It's fine. Nothing happened."

"Don't make me read between the lines, Jo."

"It's just... Robert kissed me. Maybe it was just a goodnight kiss on the cheek that landed wrong. I turned and left right away. I swear."

For a few seconds, Mela was quiet. Then she squared her shoulders. "Rob has no business kissing your cheek goodnight, Johanna," she said. "I'm sorry this happened."

"It's nothing."

"No, it isn't. It made you uncomfortable."

Johanna rubbed a hand over her cheek. "I suppose it did. But there are other reasons I'd like to go with you next time. I do have more fun working with you. And I do love the sea."

"When I go back, Jo," Mela said, "I won't be in a position to hire an assistant. Or, in fact, in a position where I need one. It's a fairly simple life up there."

"Oh. Oh." Johanna's lips pressed into a tight line. "I'm... Well, would you let me know if... Oh, well." She shook her head and laughed, but Mela saw her eyes.

"We'll see what happens," she said and took the young woman's hands, squeezing them once as if shaking on a deal. "We'll see what happens, and we'll take baby steps to get where we want to be. For starters, you can come with me to visit. We'll talk to my friends in Bay Harbor. Maybe there are opportunities you'd like to check out. But again, it's a simpler, slower life." She let Johanna's hands go.

"I would love that." Johanna stepped back and wiped her eyes. "I would love a simpler life. And you know what?"

"What?" Mela smiled.

"I didn't think the food at the gala was *that* good."

"It was very good food. It's just better when you have it on the beach," Mela said.

Johanna smiled and turned to leave. "So you will let me know?"

Mela nodded. "The moment I make a decision."

Johanna left, and as soon as the door closed, Mela sank onto her bed.

Everything was falling apart. Her backdoor career, her marriage, all that had defined her life in New Hampshire.

She herself had defined much less of her life than she'd thought. Her ship had drifted in the currents of motherhood and marriage and duty to others.

Now the kids had flown the nest, and Rob was almost where he needed to be. He was also forgetting Mela, going to the ballet, and, worst of all, kissing employees.

If Mela wanted to straighten her ship and lead the life she wanted, she had to take charge of the big decisions. She'd learned enough to know that hesitation yielded poor results. But even the big decisions started with baby steps.

Mela picked up her phone and called her husband.

CHAPTER 22

What did Mother want to tell me? I wish I could have understood her words. They were her last, so they must've been important.

"I always get sick when I read in the car," Johanna said and slowed to turn.

"I'm all right." Mela closed the journal and looked out of the window. The forest was getting sparse, and deciduous trees gave way to pines and firs and sandy soil. The afternoon sun was shining brightly on the estuaries and cranberry bogs that more and more frequently invaded the land. They were getting near the coast.

Mela had read enough of the journal to know Julie and her mother, Constance, had been close. At least until Julie, young and unmarried, found herself pregnant. It had caused a rift between mother and daughter that had deepened by Julie's decision to keep Mela's father secret. Shortly after she confided in Constance, Julie moved to the house in Bay Harbor.

Once a year on the day of her passing, Julie and Mela had picked flowers and sprinkled them in the sea, and Julie told stories about Grandma Connie. In all those stories, Constance loved Julie very much.

"Are you okay?" Johanna asked after a while.

"I'm fine," Mela said automatically.

There was a pause. Then, Johanna said, "You don't have to do that anymore, you know."

Mela looked at her. "Do what?"

"Say you're fine when you're not." Johanna smiled at her. "I don't work for you anymore, so you don't have to keep it professional."

"Oh." Mela sighed. "It's just my mother's journal entries." She patted the diary on her lap. "As a child, I didn't know how much she was carrying. I had no idea what was going on. I still don't."

"Children aren't supposed to know too much," Johanna said. "They can't fix things for their parents."

"It's just strange to find out forty years later."

"There it is." Johanna pointed to the sign saying Bay Harbor. She flicked the blinker and took the exit.

"You'll need a car of your own," Mela said. Johanna had driven the family cars. "What happens if you get bored and don't want to stay?"

"My brother will pick me up," Johanna said, distracted by merging. "But I don't have anywhere else I want to go, so I'm crossing my fingers that Bay Harbor is it for me. I want it to be."

"There's a small downtown area," Mela said. "With a handful of small stores and a couple of restaurants and coffee places."

"It sounds nice. I saved some money I should invest," Johanna said. "If I like the town, I might look into buying a place and finding work online. Plenty of personal assistants work virtually now, and I've had a couple of people ask if I'm available."

"I bet they did." Mela smiled. It was no secret that Johanna was efficient. "If you do want to buy, there are lots of empty houses." Mela had driven past them in the blue truck, wishing she could fix them as well as Julie's house. Only a handful of properties were oceanfront, but most had at least a view. "Seaside homes are expensive even in Bay Harbor, but a couple of them looked like foreclosures. If you have time to wait for the banks to turn their wheels, you could put in a bid and see if you get lucky. It can take months, though."

"I love old houses," Johanna said. "I'll look into it if I decide to stay."

They'd reached another turnoff and took it. Suddenly, beach heather covered vast areas to both sides of the street, its purple bloom broken only by the shimmering blue water of an estuary winding its way to the sea. An osprey circled and dove, but they'd passed before Mela could tell if it had caught a fish.

She let her window down. The air already tasted salty, fragrant with the scent of heather and the dry aromas of pine sap and crushed juniper berries.

Mela turned her attention back to Johanna. "You might prefer to stay at the motel," she said. "You are very welcome to stay at the house, too, but the rooms aren't furnished yet. So right now, you're looking at a less-than-twin-sized bed, a couch, or a camping mattress on the floor."

Johanna smiled at her. "I'll take the motel. But thank you."

There was a sign marking the town of Bay Harbor. Mela put a hand out of the window, letting the slipstream play with it.

She was back again.

And this time, she was back for good.

Rob had been relieved when she'd suggested the divorce. He was falling in love with someone else, he'd admitted. It caused him feelings of anger and guilt that he didn't know how to handle. Mela had asked him to apologize to Johanna and agreed that their time together was coming to an end. *Let's make it a gentle end, Rob,* she'd said. *Let's keep the memory of our time together what it was—happy. Let's stay friends.*

They both had cried at the loss of their marriage, but they both knew they were opening new doors in their lives as well. Life was full and rich and always changing. Mela knew it wasn't in anyone's power to hold on to parts of it any more than it was possible to catch a wave or a ray of light. But like water and light, love would never end.

There'd be no more mansion, no rustling gowns or heels, no bribing the kids with fancy vacations on tropical islands. Mela would never be as wealthy again as she had been married to Rob.

But she had enough.

Enough to fix up her small blue house, enough to buy bread and cheese and good wine, enough to spend her days tending honeybees and her evenings sitting with friends, looking out over the sea.

Her kids would find their way to visit themselves. Already, Kimmie had promised to come back soon.

"How did Kimmie take the news about the divorce?" Johanna asked quietly, as if she'd read Mela's thoughts.

Mela raised an eyebrow. "I'd like to claim she was surprised, but she wasn't. Maybe she saw it coming sooner than I."

"I hope I wasn't a factor. I do wish I'd kept my mouth shut."

"Not at all," Mela said. "I'm glad you told me."

Johanna nodded.

"Turn here. This is Seasweet Lane. And look—see the blue house at the end? That's it." It was as if her lungs filled with happiness instead of air. This was her house. Her place by the sea. She was going to fill it with flowers and flip-flops and friends and all the love she had to give.

"Oh, it's beautiful!" Johanna exclaimed. "Look at that view!" She parked at the curb and peered at the house and the sliver of sea that was visible.

"Isn't it?" Mela asked, savoring the joy of being back. "Isn't it the bee's knees?" She laughed at her terrible little pun and got out.

"I love it." Johanna followed Mela through the front yard. "Isn't it everyone's dream to have a house by the sea like this?"

Mela turned the key and opened the door. "I'm back," she whispered.

Welcome, said the drawings on the wall as she walked in. Welcome, said the bookshelf of childhood treasures waiting to be rediscovered, and welcome said the neglected garden behind the glass sliding door.

Mela turned to the young woman by her side. "Have a seat on the patio, my dear. The bees won't sting you. I'll get us something to drink."

Johanna, clutching her purse as if she were shy, opened the sliding door and let herself out. Mela watched as she stood looking out at the sea. Then Jo closed her eyes and turned her face to the sun, smiling a smile that came from deep inside her.

Mela dialed Amelie. "I'm back," she said.

"Took you long enough," Amelie replied. "I was starting to think you'd fallen for the glitz and glamour of a political career after all."

"You're right; I was gone for almost three days." They both laughed.

"It wasn't my career," Mela said then. "Not anymore. There are good people eager and ready to take my place, and they're a lot hungrier than I am. I had my fill. It's time to let someone else prove themselves."

"Good for you," Amelie said. "Oh shucks, good for you. I'm so happy, Mela!"

"Me, too. But Rob and I are getting divorced."

"Oh, I'm sorry. I'm here if you need to talk."

"I'll probably want to talk sometime," Mela said. "But Rob will always be in my life. Now that we're moving on, we can finally be friends again."

"That's a great attitude," Amelie said. "You sound good."

"I feel good," Mela said. "I feel a whole lot better than before. What are you up to?"

"While you were getting important things done, I was learning how to properly quarter cherry tomatoes. I used my newfound skill just now to make a lovely lemon garlic pasta with roasted tomatoes and parmesan shavings. They're starting to melt," Amelie said. "I mean, it tastes *so* good. Do you want to come over for dinner?"

Mela wanted to know why Amelie was spending so much effort cutting already small tomatoes, but there was no hurry. They had weeks and months and years to talk. "I'd love to, but I brought my assistant, Johanna, with me," she said. "Former assistant, I should say. Jo wanted to live by the sea too."

"Well, does your former assistant look like she could use some lemony, parmesan goodness and a tall glass of icy lemonade?"

Mela looked at the young woman. She was sitting on the stone wall, still gazing at the sea. In her hands was a sprig of blue salvia. Some of Julie's plants had seeded themselves out on the field, and she'd picked one.

"Yes." Mela smiled. "She definitely needs lemony goodness and a swim in the sea."

"Did she bring a suit?"

"I don't know. But we can always buy her one."

"If there's swimming, I'm coming over to yours," Amelie decided. "I'll be there in five. Set the table, girl."

She hung up, and Mela went to the patio door. "Time for dinner," she called out. "My friend Amelie is coming over."

Jo swung her legs off the wall. "Would you mind giving me a quick ride to the motel?"

It took Mela a moment to realize Jo thought she was being asked to leave. "Oh, goodness, Jo, you're eating with us. Amelie would never forgive me if I didn't keep you."

Just then, her phone rang. She checked the screen. "Peter!"

"I hear you're back in town," he said.

His formal tone made Mela smile. Almost, he'd called her Pamela. "How did Amelie tell you already?"

"Amelie is innocent," he said. "My personal balcony watch spotted you driving on Main five minutes ago. We thought we'd offer to share our mac and cheese dinner with you."

"That's kind of you, and I'd love to. But Amelie cooked and is coming over, bringing dinner to share," Mela said. "You're very welcome to join."

"What did she make?" came a voice from the background.

Mela chuckled. "Tell Sunny it's lemon pasta with perfectly quartered roasted cherry tomatoes and melting parmesan shavings."

"I'll bring our garlic bread to stretch it a little," Peter promised. "I'm glad you're back, Mela."

Mela's cheeks flushed warm. "I'm glad too," she said softly. "And I'm glad you're here. Maybe..."

"Yes?"

"Maybe we can have another ice cream together, now that I'll be living here," Mela said. "Casually, you know. To get to know each other better."

There was a pause.

"I would like that," he finally said. "Though my mind has been made up ever since you took my hand when you lost your balloon."

Another moment of silence passed. Mela didn't know what to say.

"Did you forget?" he asked. "It's a long time ago."

Sometimes, it wasn't about new doors opening. Sometimes, the best doors were old ones that had always been open. Mela took a deep breath. "I never forgot you held my hand."

"Did you forget how it felt, Mela? Because I remember the feeling."

"Me too," Mela said. "I remember it too."

"Some memories shape a heart forever," Peter said. "So that nothing else can ever quite fit it."

Mela couldn't think.

"I can hear you both, you know," Sunny said somewhere in the background.

"We'll come over, Mela," Peter said.

CHAPTER 23

Kimmie couldn't wait to get back to NYC. Now that Mom had left, Dad kept his composure as usual, but Kimmie knew he wanted time for himself.

Mom had come into Kimmie's bedroom at night, in her robe and flowing hair like a good-looking ghost. Kimmie had been wide awake, researching the next project she wanted to tackle. Or searching for it. Research came later when you knew your topic.

Sitting on the foot of Kimmie's bed in the light of a full moon, Mom had told her that she was returning to Bay Harbor. Dad wanted to stay in New Hampshire. They'd already talked with Tammy from PR, who probably was sitting at her computer as well, thinking of ways to spin the facts so they looked as golden as the moonlight.

Which maybe they were. Her parents' divorce seemed to make more sense than her own. Kimmie could tell that it allowed them to be friends instead of staying married and letting love fray into resentment.

It was good. But it made her feel even worse about the way she'd handled her own divorce.

"Do you want a cup of coffee, Dad?" She pushed the silver thermos across the breakfast table to him and then took another warm cinnamon bun. She simply couldn't resist the pecan icing.

He looked up from the papers he was reading, distracted. "Thank you, no. I'm trying to cut down."

Kimmie stood, biting into the sweet bun. "I'll give you some space, Dad. I'm developing a stress ulcer and need to get home so I can go to bed and cry over everything that's happened. My divorce, and your divorce, and all that. I'm really terribly unhappy."

Dad nodded, scribbling notes on the paper. "Have fun, honey," he muttered.

Kimmie walked past him, pressing a sugary kiss on his head before she exited the room. "Call me if it gets unbearable," she called back. "I'll try to stop crying long enough to console you."

"Alrighty, Kimster," Dad murmured and fished for his glasses. "You too. Bye."

In the hall, Jack was on his way to the dining room, carrying a small bowl with strawberries and another with freshly whipped cream. The butler was a year younger than herself but had worked for the family as long as she'd been a reporter.

She snagged a strawberry. "Keep an eye on him, Jack," she said. "Make sure he eats."

"I always do, Kimmie," Jack said. "I'll call you if anything's the matter."

"And if you could do me a favor, call my siblings and tell them to visit and keep Dad company." She gave him a professional smile.

"Yeah, I don't think I will do that." Jack lifted the berries to demonstrate. "*This* is my job. You can call your siblings yourself."

Kimmie sighed. "Worth a try," she murmured and clapped a hand on Jack's shoulder. Jack gave a hollow laugh and continued into the breakfast room. Kimmie went to pick up her bag from upstairs. Mom had called Sisley and Morris to tell them the news.

They might come to New Hampshire to check on Dad. Dad might even notice.

But now that Mom was on her own, Kim imagined even Sis and Morris would want to drive up to Bay Harbor to see their mother's new place. If they had any sense, they'd do it soon. Kimmie had enjoyed her short stay, and it'd left a lasting good impression. Both Sis and Morris could use some of that in their lives. The family tended to work too much.

She lugged her things into the trunk of her Audi and pushed them inside, then slammed the lid shut and sat behind the wheel. It was a relief to close the door.

Back to her own world. Her own apartment, own friends, own work.

Own, own, own.

Her stomach hurt a little, and she pressed a hand to her midriff. It wasn't hunger—she didn't really have an ulcer, did she? She'd just said that to get a rise out of

Dad. Maybe she should get it checked out, though. Just in case.

Kimmie started the engine. Just in case...just in case... It was like a drumbeat in her head. She was guilty of working too much herself. It had cost her a marriage. Would it cost her health as well?

She drove down the driveway. Already it was hot, but the trees still shaded the convertible. "Maybe," she murmured, looking at her reflection in the mirror, "maybe I need a nice, long vacation to get off the stress train."

She had everything she needed with her. Everything but a swimsuit.

When she got to the I-95 freeway, Kimmie passed the south ramp leading to NYC and instead took the north ramp to Maine. At the first gas station, she pulled over and filled up the tank, then folded back the convertible roof, humming under her breath. It was a beautiful day. She could go a little slower and let the wind play with her hair instead of rushing.

Just the thought of a beach vacation with Mom made her feel better. Even her stomach had stopped complaining.

She pulled forward to the little market attached to the station and went into the cool interior. Usually, she would have gone for coffee and chips, but she got herself an orange juice and unroasted almonds instead. She felt like mixing things up. Do something new. Take care of herself. Vacation with Mom. Eat leisurely dinners in the backyard. Laugh with Bennett.

She set her purchases on the counter. Of course also laugh with other people her age, if they existed in Bay Harbor. She could barely remember how hanging out with friends felt. When she wasn't traveling, she was spending too much time online.

"You having a good day?" The old man ringing her up nodded appreciatively at her face and put the almonds in a paper bag.

"Yep. You?" Where had *Bennett* come from? Kimmie ran her card.

"Every day the sun shines." The man handed her the bag. His eyes crinkled, the wrinkles a testament to frequent laughter. "Take care."

"You too." Kimmie smiled at him. "Thanks for being nice."

He winked, already helping the next customer.

She left, convinced he was nice whatever the weather was like. Some people just had a knack for enjoying life. The old man on his bike had been one of them, she felt sure. He'd left a lasting impression on her.

Kimmie got into her car, put her sunglasses on, and then she got back on I-95. The highway was empty, and she drove in the right lane. Fast enough to make progress but slow enough to enjoy her juice, the wind in her hair, and the glorious blue sky. Now and then she caught peeks of the sea, and when she did, she cheered it a little with her juice bottle, laughing at herself.

When she pulled off the highway three hours later, her ears were ringing. She stopped at a small marketplace café in Beach Cove.

"Is your coffee good?" she asked the waiter.

"It is," he said. "Though I'm biased."

Kimmie smiled. "Do you own the place?"

"I do. I can recommend the Black Forest torte. My wife baked it, and it's outstanding."

The expression on his face made Kimmie want to cry. Why couldn't she have loved her husband as much as the café owner loved his wife?

"Can I buy an entire torte?" she asked. She wanted to bring some of that love-torte with her to share with everyone in Bay Harbor.

"No," he said regretfully. "We have a strict one-piece-per-person policy when it comes to the tortes. Our fishermen call in before the sun comes up, leaving messages to reserve a slice for when they get back to the harbor. I'm not going to tango with that crowd, if you know what I mean."

Kimmie had no idea what he meant. "Tough crowd?" she guessed.

"But kind-hearted."

"I've never been to a town with a torte-rationing policy."

He had a contented expression on his face. "You should come and stay a few days."

"Maybe I will," Kimmie said. "I like a rough crowd, and I usually tango with it too." Suddenly, she wanted her next article to be about small towns. There'd be nothing much going on, she assumed, but maybe it could be a light-hearted piece for once. Or, who knew?

Maybe there was more than met the eye. "What's your name?" she asked impulsively.

"I'm Tom. If you're serious about coming here, you'll have to stay at the Beach Cove Inn. It's gorgeous, but it books out far in advance. You'll have to reserve a room well ahead of time."

"I'm Kimmie. Do you have a number?"

Tom nodded at the table beside her. Several had been pushed together to make space for five women and, in a highchair between them, a golden-haired toddler. The women were her mom's age, except a woman with sea-green eyes who held a sugar cookie for the baby.

"Mom?" Tom tapped one of the women on the shoulder. "This lady might be interested in staying at the inn. Do you have a card for her?"

"Yes." Tom's mom dug in her purse and produced a card that she handed to her son. She smiled, and the lady beside her turned her silver head. "You're welcome any time, honey," she said. "I'm Maisie, this is Ellie, and we run the inn. Give us a call, and we'll see what we can do."

Kimmie smiled back. "Thank you very much."

Small towns. She'd never considered them for her articles. But there was always interesting stuff going on when everybody knew everyone else. There were always secrets and connections and feuds to reveal.

Maybe she really would spend more time in Maine. She could make small-town mysteries her thing. It wasn't as high impact as her usual work, but it would help with the stomach ulcer situation.

The green-eyed mom suddenly frowned. Kimmie held her breath, unsure what was happening. The woman beside the mom, a pale woman with a pile of books on the table beside her, put a hand on her arm. Slowly, the seafoam eyes lost their glare. The baby gurgled happily, the fat little hands grabbing for her mother's black hair.

Tom turned to hand her the card. "Do you still want your allotted slice?" he asked politely.

"Yes, please," Kimmie said. "And whatever coffee I'm allowed. Also please."

He nodded. "Got it." Then he left.

Kimmie turned her face into the sun. The harbor was visible from the marketplace, and the sea was almost unnaturally blue.

"What a beautiful town," she murmured as if she was already dictating the beginning of her story.

One of the ladies at the table beside her replied. "Isn't it?" she said softly. "Where are you from?"

Kimmie turned. The woman was beautiful in her flowing dress and hair. Her eyes were soft and kind. "My mom just moved to Bay Harbor," she said. "I'm on my way there to visit."

"Oh, how nice," the lady said. "There's a little bakery here that sells great cakes; you could bring your mom one of those. My daughter Em bakes them herself, and if you call her now, she might be able to get you one by the time you're ready to leave. Tell her Cate gave you the number. But don't be disappointed if she can't do it. She's pregnant, and some days are more difficult than others." Cate scribbled a number on a Post-it note.

Kimmie leaned over and took it. "Thank you," she said again. "Thanks very much."

She called the number right away, but the call went to voice mail. Instead of giving the pregnant daughter more work, Kimmie said quietly, "I just wanted to let you know that your mom and your mom's friends are kind people. I hope you feel okay. All the best for the baby."

Tom arrived with a foamy, icy frappuccino and the torte. "I thought you needed something yummy," he said. "You look like you drink too much black coffee without sugar. Try something sweet for a change."

Kimmie didn't know if she should laugh or cry. "Thank you," she said finally. "Hey—are you married to the baker?"

"Yes. Why?"

Kimmie chuckled. "Just a guess. Congratulations on the baby!"

"Thank you. It'll be a ride. We just found out we're having twins. A boy and a girl." He ran a hand through his hair. "Well, enjoy."

"Thanks."

The owner's mother turned around again. "Don't worry about what he said," she said. "You go ahead and drink black coffee if you like. It's fine."

"All right," Kimmie said, and this time, she did laugh. Then she hurried to eat her torte because fishing vessels were steering into the harbor and she wasn't ready to fight the fishermen for her table.

CHAPTER 24

Amelie wiped the salt water from her eyes with a corner of her beach towel before it made her sun lotion run. "Your grandmother had a secret?"

Mela plopped down on her towel, skipping the drying. She blinked into the sky. "From what I can tell, she was hiding something from Mom. And Mom, in turn, refused to share my dad's identity. I think both their secrets came between them."

"Sounds complicated." Amelie thought of her mother, Meredith. Part of the reason why Amelie had become a psychologist was her complex relationship with Mom. The other part was that Meredith had wanted her daughter to do something medical for a career.

"I'm sure Mom and Grandma hoped they could still work it out."

"I wished they'd have gotten around to it." Amelie lay on her beach towel. It felt so good to lie on warm sand after a long swim in the sea.

It was still strange not to cover up and simply lie exposed, belly and all, on her beach towel. For years, she'd been unwilling to be seen. But the sun and the breeze felt great on her skin. And Mela seemed so comfortable. Not only with herself, but with Amelie too. Mela never looked twice and never commented, never joked. It helped.

"Would you like some blueberries? They're from the farmers market. They have the most amazing things there. I got a pound of Bing cherries and ate them all before I even got home. No wonder Mom wanted to have a stand to sell honey." Mela offered Amelie a pack of blueberries so ripe with summer sun they were shining black.

Amelie helped herself to a handful of the berries and popped a few in her mouth, where they exploded with juice and flavor. "Hmmm," she hummed contentedly. "So sweet."

"Do you have time to come buy honeybees with me?" Mela wiped the berry juice from her hands and reached for the phone in her bag. "It's eleven. I have a date with a beekeeper in an hour and a half."

Amelie took her phone and swiped for her calendar. "I'm free until five," she said. "Then I have a client stop by."

"Is that a yes? I don't want to claim all your time."

"Claim away." Amelie put her phone back and closed her eyes. "That's a yes. I only want to go grocery shopping too. Where's the beekeeper?"

"He's only a few minutes out of town," Mela said. "He's retiring and plans on moving to Florida. I get to swipe his bees and some equipment." She smiled, clearly excited at the prospect.

"Oh, lucky!" Amelie said. "Look at you!"

"Peter knew a guy who knew a guy, and I happened to be in the right spot at the right time."

Amelie wondered whether she should use the opportunity and ask about Peter.

Peter had always had a thing for Mela. He'd often mentioned her when he or Amelie brought up the topic of their childhoods. If it'd been any other guy as handsome and kind as Peter, Amelie might've been jealous. After all, Mela had seemed happily married on TV, while Amelie was right there.

But it *was* Peter, and Mela was ready to start a new life. Amelie wanted Mela to enjoy flirting with an old friend as much as she could. She'd always wished the two of them could get a second chance at love.

Mela looked at her. "Do you have clients every day?"

Amelie nodded. "I take what I can. But it's great because I can set my own schedule. I love my job."

"How about Bennett?"

Amelie closed her eyes. "He's visiting friends from his school days. I'm so glad he took a vacation."

They lay in the sun until their suits were dry, and then they packed up their beach bags and blueberries and mystery novels and went up to the house.

"I'm going home to change," Amelie announced and pulled a dress over her head. "I need a shower."

"I'll pick you up in an hour?" Mela brought her to the front door.

"Great." Amelie looked back as she left the blue house. She didn't want to leave. Even as a child, she'd preferred the beach house over her own. Her family's house was bigger, but it wasn't by the sea. And there was something about the blue house that made her feel so welcome and warm... Just like Julie had been welcoming and warm. Now it was Mela, doing the same.

Already almost to the gate, Amelie stopped and looked back. "Are these empty houses in the street vacation homes? Or are they for sale?"

Mela leaned against the door frame. "Johanna told me this morning that some of them at least are for sale. Why?" She smiled. "Are you thinking of moving?"

"Maybe," Amelie said, surprising herself. "I might have a look at them. I don't know why it never occurred to me before. But it's a buyer's market right now, and sooner or later the houses will get snatched up."

"It doesn't hurt to have a look. I could see you being my neighbor in a nice house with a big kitchen and a garden looking out at the sea."

"You had me at big kitchen." Suddenly, Amelie felt inspired. She really should have a look. There had been years when every single house on the street had been firmly in a family's hands. But the market had been up and down lately. A lot of people had put up their vacation homes for sale. And there had even been a handful of foreclosures.

"Johanna has an appointment with a realtor tomorrow," Mela said. "I'm sure she doesn't mind if you tag along. Or you can get your own realtor if you're serious."

"I'll think about it."

She waved, and then she went home to shower and change. After she'd dried her short curls, she put on the new, lemon yellow dress made from locally sourced linen. It was new and exciting to put on. She'd admired it forever without allowing herself to buy it because when would she wear it? Did she *need* something as frivolous as a yellow linen dress?

For weeks, every time she'd gone into the little boutique, she'd touched the dress. She admired the happy color and the cute cut that was so perfect for her curvy figure. She'd breathed a sigh of relief that nobody else had bought the dress, either. Then, Mela's pretty swimsuits taught her a lesson. If a piece of fabric gave you back something as big as the courage to be seen, it was worth purchasing.

Now, Amelie permitted herself to treat herself now and then. Two days after buying the swimsuits, she'd gone back to the boutique. Cheeks flushed with excitement, she'd splurged on her yellow dress.

Amelie turned in the mirror. It looked fantastic. And with her new tan from going swimming with Mela every day, it looked even better.

A horn honked outside.

Amelie grabbed her straw hat and hurried downstairs. She'd love to see an old beekeeper sell Mela his equipment. Amelie laughed at being so invested in the outcome, slapped her sun hat on, and closed the front door.

CHAPTER 25

The more I think about it, the more I wonder what Mother saw when she looked at me with those faraway eyes of hers.

"That's more than you need for keeping backyard bees, young woman." The old man pushed his ball cap back and scratched his forehead. "I mean, I'm happy to sell it to you, but what are you going to do with it?"

"I'm not sure yet." Mela let her gaze wander over the white wooden boxes, the cartons with their narrow frames and grids and tools. She reached out and touched the honey extractor. It smelled so sweet and yummy she wanted to tuck it under her arm right then and there. Of course, the metal drum was much too big and unwieldy.

Hoping she could bring some bee things home right away, Mela had borrowed Peter's pickup truck. Johanna had asked to borrow Mela's car to go house hunting, so it had worked out well. "I think I can fit it all in my shed."

"But how many colonies do you want to set up?" he asked. His bushy mustache wiggled with curiosity under the bulbous nose.

"Three, for starters," Mela said and smiled. That would fill the backyard hives she had cleaned out and ready to house new colonies. "And then a hundred more."

"In your *backyard*?" He shook his head. "The neighbors won't thank you for that. Besides, unless you have one heck of a backyard, it's not allowed."

"Well, I'll just have to rent a field," Mela declared.

"Oh," Amelie said, interested. "That's new."

"I've always wanted a field by the sea." Mela rubbed her sunburned shoulder. "And I would love to sell seaside honey at the farmers market."

"You would find plenty of buyers, too. But you'll need a lot of hives to make money from honey," the old man warned. "Selling bees is less work, and the orchards will pay you if you rent them colonies in spring. Maintaining the bees and equipment is a lot of work, and you'll need a strong back. You'll have to buy more colonies, too. I only have a handful left now."

"Hmm. Well, baby steps," Mela decided. "I'll take what you can part with. It's a great deal and a lot cheaper than buying everything new."

"That's true," the beekeeper agreed. "And if you decide to stick to a couple of hives in your backyard, you can always sell again what you don't need."

"Where did you keep your colonies?" Amelie asked.

"I do have a field. It's even by the sea." The old man smiled. "It's been in my family for almost a century. Nobody would buy that sort of property for beekeeping now, only for building. But no thanks to that. There are enough empty houses already." He thoughtfully patted an empty hive. "I learned everything I know about honeybees out there, and it's served my family well. Even my son's a beekeeper."

"That's lovely," Mela said. Maybe if her mother had lived, her life would have gone a completely different route as well. Surely the two of them would have met the other beekeepers in the area.

The old man shrugged thoughtfully. "He moved to California for a girl, but she skipped out on him. My wife hoped he'd find his way back home, but there's good money for a beekeeper in the big almond orchards out west. He does well for himself, but we hope that he'll come back to Bay Harbor one day."

"You wouldn't sell me your field, would you?" Mela asked suddenly.

"I thought we were taking baby steps," Amelie said, exasperated.

The old man leaned on the tower of hives. "I want my son to have the field someday."

"Of course. I just thought I'd give it a try." Mela smiled. She wanted a field, but she loved a parent who loved their child even more. "That's beautiful, especially when the property has been in the same family for so long."

"Well, it's too cold in the winters for my wife here now." The old man sighed. "I'll do what I can to keep her comfortable while I'm lucky enough to have her with me." Again his mustache moved, and he weaved his head. "I'll tell you what, we can help each other. The bees are already in the field. You can buy them from me. I'm keeping ownership of the field, but if you mow it once or twice a year and keep some bees on it, you can use it for free until my son or I come back to Bay Harbor. I also have a barn and a tractor. I don't mean to sell either since they belong to this house, but you are welcome to use them."

Mela clapped her hands together, her cheeks flushing warm with excitement. "Are you sure?" she asked the beekeeper at the same time Amelie asked her, "Are you sure?"

They all laughed.

"Well, you girls go and decide on it," the beekeeper said. "I have someone else interested in the equipment, and I'll show it to him because I said I would. But he's only visiting from Vermont. My bees like making Bay Harbor honey, and I like to think they'll stay on my field. Give me a call by tomorrow and let me know if we have a deal."

"Can we look at the field?" Amelie asked. "We can drive by on our way home if you let us know where it is."

"Sure." The beekeeper drew them a map. The pencil looked tiny in his wide, hard hands. Amelie wondered whether Mela knew what she was doing. She was going on fifty, and heaving hives around sounded like labor.

The beekeeper gave them each a jar of honey as a parting gift.

In the truck, Amelie turned the glass. The sun made it glow golden amber. "It looks precious," she said.

"It is. Not only does it taste good, but it also has healing properties." Mela flicked the blinker even though the street was empty and turned into a field lane.

It wasn't paved, and she slowed down. The truck bumped happily over shallow divots and small rocks on ground the summer sun had baked solid. The lane was fringed with grass, wildflowers, and a sprinkle of thick oaks with sprawling branches that provided puddles of shade. "Don't worry, Amelie. He's only got twenty-five hives. It'll be my hobby to take care of them."

Amelie didn't look convinced. "How many do you need to make a living from beekeeping?"

"It depends."

"On what?"

"Mostly on what you sell. There's honey, but also the pollen bees collect, wax for candles, propolis, which is a sort of resin, and royal jelly, which is what larvae are fed to turn them into queens. And of course bees themselves, if you have some to spare."

"So how many colonies to make a living, do you think? Ten? Twenty-five? Give me a ballpark number."

Mela had researched the topic already, sitting on her patio the night before with a glass of strawberry lemonade and her laptop on her knees. She'd bought potted night-blooming jasmine to go with Peter's lavender tree, and the warm night air had smelled good enough that she'd wanted to bottle it. "Some say upward of two hundred; others say five hundred plus." She smiled at her friend.

"Five hundred?" Amelie stared back. "Mela, stop it. No wonder he asked whether you had a strong back."

Mela checked the map the old man had given her. "I'm not looking for a full-time job, Amelie. I'm looking to live my dream. Selling honey at the farmers market is on my bucket list."

"Yours or Julie's?"

Mela laughed. "Mine, but Julie put it there, so it belongs to both of us. I'm determined to sell honey on the market, even if it's only one jar. Then I'll buy flowers with the money and scatter them on the sea."

"That's a beautiful tribute to your mom, Mela." Amelie sounded mollified. "Have you just thought of it?"

"I don't know. It popped into my mind just now. But Julie and I used to scatter flowers on the sea for Grandma. You should think..." Mela gripped the steering wheel tighter. "I should have thought to do it earlier, but it never occurred to me."

"You can bring her flowers now," Amelie said. "I think it's a wonderful idea to make it a tradition."

Mela slowed to a crawl. "I think this is it." She parked, and they got out.

Behind the alley of oaks lay the field. At the end was a shallow drop-off overlooking the sea, and to the side, low hedges of bush-honeysuckle, witch hazel, and winterberry formed boundaries to wheat fields. The beekeeper had told Mela they used to belong to his family but were sold a long time ago to a working farm. His field was the only one full of wildflowers. Framed by golden wheat swaying in the breeze, it was an image to widen the heart.

It was barely noticable driving by. A flash of blue and green and yellow, and it had passed.

But for those who slowed, the view was like a summer kiss.

They stood, soaking it all in while the sun warmed their backs.

"I feel like I'm standing in a picture book," Mela said finally and put a hand to her heart. "How can a simple field be so pretty?"

"Look at the *colors*." The grass had been hayed and grown back to knee height. Amelie pointed. "I recognize the tall blue and pink lupines, the fluffy white ones are Queen Anne's lace, the clouds of tiny white daisies are fleabane. And that's pink meadowsweet, and I think purple fireweed."

Mela tried to memorize the names of the plants. She, too, knew a few, but there many more here; yellow and purple and red and blue, scattered everywhere. She wanted to wade through the grass and pick them all into one enormous bouquet to brighten the kitchen.

"Here." Mela fished a straw hat and veil from the backseat of the truck. "We're going in."

Amelie looked at the veil. "Your backyard bees are one thing. They are well away from where we sit. This is different, Mela. This is twenty-five hives of bees that aren't used to visitors. Has it occurred to you that they may not appreciate us trampling their flowers?"

"It's fine. We'll be careful. We won't trample very much."

She pulled a smoker from a box on the truck bed and puffed it a few times because it was impossible to hold a smoker and not puff it.

Amelie shaded her eyes against the sun and squinted at her friend. "I guess it's time to confess, Mela."

"Confess what?" Mela had already put on her hat and was slipping the veil over it, cinching it tight so no bees could get in. The wide brim kept it away from her face. "Better put your veil on. Just in case."

Amelie took it but didn't put it on. "Yes...see, just-in-case is a problem."

Mela dropped her arms. Amelie had sat on her patio while honeybees busily hummed in the air. It couldn't be, could it? "Come on, Amelie," she pleaded.

Amelie shrugged. "Yes, I'm afraid so. I'm scared of getting stung."

CHAPTER 26

Honeybees keep no secrets. The queen hides nothing from her daughters. The night before I had to pack Mom's things, I was lying on her bed, crying. I got a tissue from the drawer and found the photo.

Mela lifted two glasses and the large insulated bottle from her basket and poured. "Here." She handed Sunny the tall glass. "It's a summer melon slushie. A little bird told me you like iced watermelon."

"I wish you were my daughter, hon." Sunny took it with both hands. "Come sit with me."

There were two chairs on the old lady's balcony this afternoon. Earlier, Mela had taken Sunny to the big-box store on the far side of town. Mela needed to stock her pantry now that she was living in Bay Harbor for good. While they were there, she'd spotted bistro sets with foldable chairs and a small mosaic table to put a coffee cup and a book on. Mela had snagged one set for Sunny's narrow balcony at the motel and one for herself to put by the stone wall at her house. She'd also ordered a nice, big wicker patio set with fluffy pillows that were as soft as a dream and would keep Sunny comfortable in Seasweet Lane.

Mela had dropped off Sunny, the bistro set, and a hot wagonwheel pizza bubbling with golden cheese at the motel because Sunny had had a lunch date with Peter. Back at home, she'd put away the groceries and gone swimming. The seawater had been deliciously refreshing after the busy stores, and she swam until she felt like the shopping trip had happened in a different universe.

Mela liked letting the sun dry her while lying on her beach towel. Lazily flipping on her phone through recipes for virgin summer drinks, she'd found the melon slushie recipe and immediately had wanted to try it out since she'd brought home a watermelon the size of a small barrel. Once she was back, showered and had made herself a tall glass of fresh orange juice, she'd cut it up and prepared the slushie for Sunny. On a roll, Mela had also prepared plates of prosciutto bites and smoked bacon jalapeños poppers for an afternoon snack.

When she'd arrived at Sunny's, the old lady was sitting on the balcony. Peter had stuffed her chair with extra pillows for comfort, and it looked like a little throne. She was dressed in a golden robe and headband that had been another shopping trip find. The afternoon sun set it aglow, and Mela had to smile when she saw her friend.

"Was the pizza good?" she inquired.

"It was incredible," Sunny said contentedly. "Though Peter ate most of it. I'm hungry again."

"Did he really? Well, I brought snacks." Mela peeled the foil wrap off the plates, releasing the full, warm scents that went well with the iced fruit, and set them on the table. "Cheers," she said and raised her glass. "It was a beautiful day, wasn't it? I had such a good time with you, my dear. We should do this more often." She sat on the chair.

"Cheers," Sunny said and adjusted her headband. "I don't think I've had this much fun since I moved here."

A small tendril of aromatic cigarillo smoke rose from the backyard. "I can hear you, you know," Peter said dryly. "I've taken you to the stores plenty of times." A bird squawked and rustled in the jasmine.

"Cheers down there," Mela called out. "He's got a drink too," she confided in Sunny. "I left a pitcher on the reception counter."

"I have a glass as well," Johanna's voice came from behind the privacy screen of Mela's old room. "Cheers."

"Cheers," everybody said back in unison, and Mela drank.

"I wanted to show you something, hon," Sunny said and set her glass down, wiping the condensation off her fingers on her robe. "I dug this out today." She lifted a slim photo album from her lap and laid it on the table. "We didn't have cell phones like today, so I don't have very many snapshots of your mom. But there are a couple."

"That's amazing, Sunny," Mela said. "I'd love to see them. I only have five photos of her since she was the one taking them."

Sunny opened the booklet. "Look." She turned the album so Mela could see. "My parents."

Mela leaned forward expectantly. The faces looking back at her were soft with age and kind, but they looked nothing like Sunny's. The photograph was black and white and yellowed from age, but the shapes of heads and chins and eyes held no familiarity.

"You don't take after them," Mela said.

"Oh, I wouldn't," Sunny said. "I was adopted."

"I had no idea." Mela looked up and smiled. "I was adopted too."

Sunny shook her head. "Goodness, child, I was so upset that they took you away. I tried to get you. They wouldn't hear of it because I'd lost my husband to a work accident. But I wished I could've had you. I tried for a long time."

"Thank you," Mela said awkwardly. "I had no idea there was someone out there looking for me."

"Were you with good people?" Sunny's voice wavered.

Mela reached out and put her hand on Sunny's. "I was. There were rough spots, but I was always with kind people. And the best of them adopted me."

They were both quiet. Mela wondered how it would have been to grow up in Sunny's house.

Eventually, Sunny sighed. "Every time I went down to the beach, I looked. I still do, though I barely get to go to the beach anymore."

"Oh, Sunny."

"Anyways." Sunny flipped a couple of pages. All Mela could see was a flash of wedding gowns and stiff backs. "This is your mom here."

Julie was sitting in a yellow bikini on a cliff, holding her knees and laughing into the camera. Her hair was windswept, and she looked happy. "When was that?" Mela asked, touching the clear wrap protecting the photo.

"That was the summer after you two moved here," Sunny answered. "I think? Yes. We met the year before."

"How did you meet?"

Sunny smiled. "We bought the same dress at the store and stood behind each other in the checkout line. First, we got to talking, and then she asked if I wanted to share her sandwiches for lunch. We went to the beach and sat in the sand. I had a thermos of tea, and she had cheese and cucumber sandwiches, so we shared and talked until it was time to get back to work."

"That sounds lovely."

"It was. We liked each other right away. I still have the dress. Sort of, anyway. It's in my house, so I can't exactly get to it."

The sun had started to go down, and Mela went to switch on the balcony light so they could see better.

There were more photos of Julie, some with Mela. In one, Julie was holding her hand; in another, Julie was sitting on the sand, hugging Mela to her. Mela was grinning into the camera, waving a Barbie doll.

"Mom looks happy," Mela murmured.

"That's because she was. She had you and a house and bees to keep busy. She worked at Bay Port University too, to make some money. She enjoyed the work, but she liked spending time with you better."

Johanna's balcony door opened and closed. Below, Peter had left already. Now and then, a soft banging came from the shed.

"I think something weighed on her." Mela told Sunny about the journal entries about Grandma Constance. She held her breath, hoping Sunny would know more about what had happened.

"She never talked about it," Sunny said thoughtfully. "I knew there was a bit of friction with her parents, but I figured it was because Julie had a baby and no husband. It wasn't unheard of back then, but it was still talked about in small towns."

Mela cleared her throat. She didn't like to think she'd been a major source of trouble in Julie's short life. "I'm glad she had you for a friend."

"She wasn't lonely," Sunny agreed. "She had me and her brother. Most of all, Julie had you girls to keep her on her toes."

"Luckily, she and Amelie's mom took turns watching us."

"Yes—what was her name again?"

"Constance. Constance Cobb." Mela smiled. "I was always a little worried she didn't approve of me, but now that I think back, she was probably just stricter than Mom."

There were a couple more photos in the album. Uncle Finn was in one, standing proudly beside the unfinished boat. Mela hadn't seen her uncle's face in years. She studied it. Finn hadn't lived in Bay Harbor, only visiting in the summers.

Sunny took out the best shots of Julie and Mela and handed them to her. Then she closed the book. "When I'm gone, you can have all the other photos as well," she said.

"Thank you very much, Sunny. It means a lot to see her." Mela sat back down. She was glad Sunny had been able to save her pictures. "It's a wonder you managed to grab the album when the landslide happened."

"It was pure instinct," Sunny admitted. "I have more albums of course, but this one happened to be on my nightstand."

"Have you asked about getting them back?"

"Of course I have. But the county said no. It's all right; it's just a bunch of stuff. I'm not about to risk one of those charming young firefighters to get them back. They stop by to chat now and then, though they pretend they're coming to see Peter." She tasted her melon slushie and popped a bacon jalapeño popper into her mouth.

"I found Julie's journal," Mela said suddenly. "It was under her bed pillow."

"A journal?" Sunny smiled as she chewed. "That's right, she used to keep one. Well, did you read it? Does she answer all your questions herself?"

Mela closed the photo album. "I'm savoring it like a special treat. I've flipped through it looking for names and pictures, but I'm only reading a few entries a day so I can do it mindfully. It's a little like meeting her, and it won't be the same the second time around. Would you like to see the journal?"

"Oh." Sunny blinked. "Well, if you'd like to share."

"She wrote about you. She liked you very much."

Sunny sighed. "The sweetheart."

Mela pulled the journal from the bag she'd slung over her chair. She flipped to a page where Julie described a trip to the area's farmers markets with Sunny. They'd made inquiries on how to have a honey stand.

Sunny read it carefully, like Mela taking her time. "I'd forgotten about this, but it was a fun afternoon. I didn't have the easiest time of it with my husband back then, so I was glad to get out of the house." She closed the journal to hand it back, snagging the last page and flipping it open. "Oh. What was that?"

Julie had pinned a baby photo to the inside of the back cover. A chubby face was looking straight into the camera.

"It's Mom as a baby." Mela smiled fondly. "Looks almost like me, but that little dress is definitely from the sixties."

Slowly, Sunny tapped her finger next to the picture. "Honey, that's not your mom."

Chapter 27

She looks like me. But I don't think it's me.

"Yes, it's Mom." Mela pulled the journal toward her. "Yes. Look at it! Look at the eyes."

Instead of looking, Sunny flipped to the front of her photo album and turned it so Mela could see. "It's not Julie."

There were three photos next to each other, carefully preserved under thin, plastic film. In each, the same baby in the same plaid baby doll dress sat in a backyard, propped up on pillows because she was too little to sit on her own.

"Mela, it's *me*."

"What?" Mela laid the journal beside Sunny's pictures. There was no doubt it was the same child.

"I still have the dress," Sunny said. "My adoptive mother sewed it herself from a Butterick pattern."

"The photo was taken in our backyard," Sunny said. "How did Julie get it?"

"I think she found it in Constance's nightstand. But I'm not sure that's the real question here," Mela murmured. Her heart was drumming in her chest. "Sunny, how come you looked like my mom as a baby? How come you looked like *me*?" She flipped to another page in the journal.

Julie had pasted in a photo of Grandma Constance, holding baby Julie up to the camera. The similarities were striking. "I was *sure* it was her," she said, non-plussed. "How is this possible?"

"I don't know." Sunny laid a veined hand on her cheek, her eyes going back and forth between the pictures. "I'm confused."

"I'm confused too." Mela sank back, staring at Sunny. Then, suddenly, she snapped up the journal. She carefully wiggled off the paperclip the salty air had rusted into place. Then she peeled the picture off the page and flipped it over. There were faint pencil marks.

"What does it say? Anything?"

Mela squinted. "I think it says June. Yeah. June. Just the month the picture was taken."

"June? Really?" Sunny held out a hand that was shaking a little. Mela handed her the photo. "Go get my reading glasses, my dear. They're on my nightstand."

Mela did, and Sunny put them on. "Those are Mother's morning glories flowering by the shed in the back," she said. "She grew them from seeds, and they never once in my life bloomed before August." She shook her head. "My middle name is June. I'm Sunny June Gardiner."

Mela reached for her hand. "Sunny June? Really? How come I didn't know that?" The nerves fluttering in her stomach made her laugh.

Sunny fiddled with the beaded chain of her reading glasses trying to untangle it. "Do you mention your second name to strangers for no reason?"

"If I was called Sunny June, I probably would. I like it."

Sunny shook out the last kink in the chain and stared at it as if she was hoping to find another. "I didn't know I was adopted until I was a teenager. Mom said she didn't know who my biological parents were."

"You never tried to find out?" It was a rhetorical question... Mela didn't dare to state what both of them were thinking. That they were related. That by some miracle, they belonged together.

"How would I have done that?" Sunny absentmindedly wrapped the chain around her thumb. "The internet wasn't invented when I had time and energy to wonder about it. I did google myself a few years ago, but...there was nothing. And anyway, I figure it's too late now."

Mela reached for Sunny's glasses and gently tugged the chain off the thumb that was starting to turn red. She set them on the table. "They have all sorts of genetic testing these days, my dear. Plus, you might have some papers from the adoption agency, no?"

"I have a few folders with papers my parents left. Anything financial was handled by their lawyer, so I never had a reason to look through the rest." Sunny folded her hands. “The boxes are in my basement, Mela. I can’t get to them now.”

“June and Julie. Same face, same eyes...” Mela stood, and then she sat again. “Are you my aunt, Sunny?” she asked. “Are you Julie’s older sister?”

“I don’t know, honey. I really don’t.”

They looked at each other.

“It’s possible,” Mela said finally. “When were you born?”

“June 1952,” Sunny said. “And Julie?”

“July 1954,” Mela said. “The same year Constance married Grandpa.”

“It’s possible Constance had me out of wedlock and was forced to give me up for adoption.” Sunny picked up her melon slushie. “I might need something stronger than melon slushie tonight, Mela.”

“I have lemonade,” Peter called out.

“Hey! I thought you were in the shed!” Mela called back.

“No, that’s the neighbor. He’s fixing his lawnmower.”

“So you heard everything?” Mela didn’t know whether she should protest or laugh.

There was a short pause.

“No?” Peter said finally. “Yes. I thought you knew I was sitting here.”

“Okay.” Mela shook her head at herself. “I guess it’s not a secret.”

“I heard you too, you know,” Johanna piped up. “I’m still here, knitting. It’s impossible not to overhear.”

"I wondered what that clicking was," Sunny said. "I thought it was my jaw."

"I didn't know you *knit*," Mela said. Johanna liked high-adrenaline sports like rock climbing and cave spelunking.

"I don't. It looks horrible." A hand appeared around the privacy wall, showing a scrunched-up patch of knotted wool.

"It gets easier," Sunny said encouragingly. "Relax your fingers."

"I'm going to get us a bottle of wine," Mela announced and stood. "The market is still open."

"I have wine too," Peter said from downstairs. "Is red good?"

"Yes," Sunny said. "And cheese crackers, please. I ate all the snacks." She picked up the last prosciutto bite and popped it in her mouth.

Peter mumbled something about doctors and diet, but they heard him leave. A few minutes later, he knocked on their door. "Little help? My hands are full."

Mela went to let him in. By now, night had fallen. The balcony light was on, but the room was dark.

Peter stood in the open door, bottle and glasses in one hand, the requested plate with cheese and crackers in the other. "Are you okay?" he murmured.

Mela nodded. She wanted to lean on him and let her head rest on his shoulder. He smelled of the garden, cigarillo, the blue truck; reliable, warm, comforting.

Holding her gaze, Peter lowered his head slowly. "Yes," he said softly, and Mela knew he wasn't asking how she was anymore.

She nodded again, and his lips brushed against her forehead. Just once, just lightly.

He straightened, and for a while, they simply looked at each other.

Then he smiled. "Can I come in?"

Mela smiled back and opened the door wider. He followed her through the small room and onto the balcony, setting down the glasses.

"I found a bottle of champagne," he announced and held up the bottle. "Just the thing for a family reunion."

"We don't know that yet," Sunny said and looked at Mela. "We only have the photo."

As if the warmth of his lips had melted her shock, light suddenly filled Mela. "We do know, Sunny," she said and held out her hands. "You're Julie's sister. You're my aunt, and I'm your niece. I can feel it. I think I can even see it."

Sunny took her hands, looking up. Tears shimmered in her eyes, and she blinked them away. "You're my niece," she murmured. "Oh, honey. Do you think?"

"I do."

"Then I've found you after all." Sunny struggled to her feet and pulled Mela into a long, warm hug.

Mela closed her eyes and let herself sink into the embrace. It almost felt like hugging Julie herself.

Suddenly, the champagne bottle popped behind them, and they broke apart, both of them simultaneously crying and laughing at their tears. Peter handed them glasses foaming with bubbles and fetched the box of tissues from Sunny's bathroom.

They sat, and Mela dabbed her cheeks while Sunny blew her nose. Peter leaned against the balcony railing between them and lifted his glass. "Congratulations." He smiled at Mela, and then he leaned over and kissed Sunny's cheek. "I couldn't be happier for you," Mela heard him murmur.

Until deep into the night, Mela and Sunny swapped stories and memories while Peter refilled glasses and periodically replenished the cheese plate. Mela was too excited and happy to think about much else, but she noted that the fourth glass on the table stayed empty and dry.

Between sips of champagne and remembering the past, Mela made a mental note. Tomorrow, she would find out why Johanna had left after she'd heard the good news.

CHAPTER 28

Kimmie looked at her mom, who was sitting across from her at the small bistro table on the sidewalk. She couldn't quite believe what she'd just heard. "Sunny is your aunt? I have a new—what, like a great-aunt?"

"I'm sure Sunny's my aunt. It all makes sense."

Kimmie broke off a corner of her croissant.

"Everything all right?" The young waitress hurried over. "They're fresh out of the oven. Do you prefer one that's not filled with marzipan?"

Kimmie hadn't noticed she'd crumbled the bread into pieces. She shook the buttery crumbs off her hand. "No, this one's great. I just... Could I have another cappuccino? Make it a strong one, please."

"I think they're always the same." The teen blinked, a little unsure. "It comes out of the machine like that."

Mela chuckled. "Whatever comes out of the machine is great. I'm enjoying mine very much. Thank you."

"Oh, okay." The waitress looked relieved, and for a moment, the sun glinted on her braces as she smiled. She left to carry out the errand.

"Such a lovely little place, isn't it?" Mela looked around contentedly. "And it's close to Amelie's house. I'll be coming here often. The apple strudel is delicious."

Kimmie eyed the flaky pastry on her mother's plate. "Isn't it a little early for ice cream?"

"It's so perfect." Mom gathered a little of each pastry, cinnamon-apple-walnut filling, vanilla ice cream, and whipped cream on her fork. "Try it."

Kimmie laughed and opened her mouth. "Mmh." It *was* delicious. As usual, her mother was right. "Mom," she said, still chewing. "There's like a whole list of things we should talk about."

"Okay." Mom looked unbothered. "Shoot."

"First," Kimmie said, trying to sound stern, "I do want a strong coffee. A shot of espresso would have done it."

"In your cappuccino?" Mom looked surprised. "Is that a thing now?"

"I don't know. But if I'll live here, which I'm thinking about, you shouldn't answer for me when I order." Boundaries were so important. Kimmie squared her shoulders.

Mom beamed at her. "I'm so happy to hear you're thinking about moving to Bay Harbor, my precious girl." She patted Kimmie's hand. "You're right about ordering. Only the poor girl was confused, and you're drinking too much coffee anyway. You'll get an ulcer."

Kimmie slouched back into her chair. "Fine. Touché." The ulcer—imaginary or not—didn't need a second cappuccino. Let alone espresso.

"Mom, I meant to ask. Are you sad about the divorce? Do you miss Dad?"

Mom glanced at her. "I do miss Dad," she said. "I miss him like I miss a good friend. But we came to a fork in our paths. We can each walk where our road takes us, or one of us must follow the other. We found that following—or being followed, for that matter—doesn't work so well for either one of us."

"How does Dad feel about his path?"

"Pretty good, I think. He seems to know where he wants to go."

"You two aren't mad at each other?"

"It was a bit of a relief to sort this out, to be honest. The painful part was admitting to myself that for years, I followed Dad on a road that didn't lead where I wanted to go. But I caught my exit when it came along. I'll be as happy here as Dad is in New Hampshire."

Highway-analogies aside, her parents were dealing with their divorce in a much more mature way than Kimmie had dealt with hers. "So what about Christmas?" she asked quickly.

Mom smiled. "We might all get together for the day, no? I think the biggest problem is to get *you* to make time for *us*." She raised an eyebrow. "I know it's still strange, my dear. But if your Dad finds love again, or if I do... I think that's good. I hope you do, too."

"I'm an adult, Mom," Kimmie said. "A divorced woman. Of course it would be good, as long as you don't fall for a gold digger. They sometimes go after rich elderly ladies."

"Oh goodness, your confidence is overwhelming." Mom pointed the fork at Kimmie. "I'll leave your coffee orders to yourself, and you'll leave me to handle my gold diggers."

Kimmie leaned back. "Last, but not least, your new aunt. Sunny."

"Yes." Unbothered, Mom finished the last of her decadent breakfast.

"You guys have no actual evidence that you are related, do you?"

"Well, we don't have a hundred percent proof, but Julie had a baby photo of Sunny in her journal. She mentioned finding a photo in Constance's nightstand, and I think it was June, also known as Sunny."

Kimmie's investigative instinct reared its head. "In my professional opinion, a resemblance is pretty weak evidence, Mom. All babies look the same, no? Where did the photo come from?"

Mom shrugged. "I don't know. Sunny's adoptive mom must have shared the photo with Constance, or maybe with the agency, and someone in the agency took pity on Constance. If it'd been me who had to give you up for adoption, I'd put heaven and earth in motion to know you're okay. A photo would be everything."

"I can't even imagine," Kimmie said.

"The only clues left might be buried in Sunny's basement boxes, and she can't get to them. Also, it doesn't matter. Both Sunny and I know."

The waitress brought the cappuccino. It had a creamy heart on top and three Amaretti cookies artfully arranged on the saucer. Kimmie smiled her thanks and took a sip. "You could do a genetic test if you wanted to know for sure," she suggested. "They're fast and easy to do these days."

Mom nodded. "I thought about it. Go ahead and order some, if you like." She turned her face into the sun, looking at peace. "Feeling better, darling? Or do you have more questions?"

"No. I'm sorry. Thanks for letting me go on a bit." Kimmie drank her cappuccino and ate her almond croissant while she ordered the tests on her phone. Now that she'd gotten her questions off her chest... It didn't matter whether Sunny was related or not. It'd be nice to have a great-aunt, fake or not.

"Are you really thinking about moving here?" Mom took a sip of ice water.

"It'd be a good investment to buy a house right now, and I'd love to spend the summers here. I have enough money for a down payment."

"So you like Bay Harbor?"

Kimmie stretched luxuriously. "Who could resist? I don't understand why there are empty houses at all."

"Sunny said a lot of people who work in Bay Port moved to Sandville when they built the new residential areas there," Mela said. "The houses are more modern, and it saved the commute to work. At the same time, a few vacation homes have come on the market. It's a good time to buy, and Dad and I are happy to help with the down payment if you want us to."

Kimmie gave her mother a grateful glance. "I hope I can do it on my own, but thank you, Mom. I might take you up on it. Apropos, do you like Johanna's real estate agent?"

"He seems capable. I can ask Johanna for his number." Mela looked thoughtfully at the sliver of sea visible at the end of the street. "Have you heard from Johanna today?"

"No, but I wouldn't expect to. It's still so early. Why?"

"No reason. Are you done? I'm going to stop by Amelie's to say good morning. You're welcome to join me."

Bennett would be there. And Kimmie wanted to see Bennett more than she liked. She wasn't ready to fall in love. "I think I'll drive around and look at houses," she said. "And, oh my goodness, I can't believe I'm saying this, but..." She grinned.

"What?"

"I think I might get in my swimsuit, take a towel, and go laze around on the beach. Maybe I'll take a book. Maybe not."

"Fabulous idea, my dear. Enjoy yourself." Mom put a bill on the table, weighing it down with her mug so the breeze wouldn't claim it, and then she rose.

Mom looked twenty years younger in her simple white linen dress and wedges, the cute straw hat on the open hazel hair, the barely-there biscuit-tan.

Kimmie stood, too. She had asked for Grandma Julie's off-shoulder '80s dress, and Mom had laughed and given it to her. The sun felt amazing on her bare neck, and the vintage skirt played around her ankles, making her feel like a boho princess. "I can't believe I have an entire summer day ahead of me to do as I like."

"I hope you're not getting distracted by your phone, and actually do take it off," Mom said.

"All of it, every last minute," Kimmie promised. "I haven't even opened my laptop since I got here."

"You needed a break," Mom said. "I'm glad Bay Harbor makes you want to take one. It has that effect on me, too."

Kimmie nodded. "Are you going to check on the bees this afternoon?"

"Yes. I opened a couple of the new hives last night and peeked inside. They have too much honey."

Kimmie slung her new striped beach bag over her shoulder. "How can bees have too much honey?"

"Darling," Mom said, "I need to teach you how to care for bees. Do you want to come watch?"

Thinking about the field of wildflowers and Grandma Julie, Kimmie suddenly felt a connection that gave her a jolt of excitement. "I do want to. But will we get stung? I'm not worried, just...asking."

"Yes." Mela smiled. "Sooner or later, we'll get stung. When it happens, I can show you a trick to make it better. If it happens enough, your body gets used to it. Then a sting feels like a pinprick, and it won't swell, either." They walked down the street to where Kimmie had parked her Audi. "It can be your new adrenaline kick." Mela put on her sunglasses. "Is that what they call it?"

"I don't think so," Kimmie said. "But I do want to come. I'll see you at the field. Text me when you leave?"

"I will. It's the first field up on the cliff," Mela answered and blinked into the sun. "If you're leaving from the house, turn right at the wishing well, past the house with the maple tree, and you can't miss it."

Kimmie opened the driver's door. "It doesn't *sound* like an adrenaline kick," she said. "Turning right at the wishing well isn't very nerve-racking."

"Good." Mom smiled.

Ulcer-wise, Kimmie had to agree. She leaned on the roof. "Where did you say they sell swimsuits?"

"It's the little boutique on Main and Perry Road. You can't miss it, darling. I think it opens at ten. Enjoy yourself!" Mom waved, and Kimmie blew her kiss back.

When she was alone, Kimmie checked the time. She still had an hour and a half until the store opened, and Bay Harbor was small. It was plenty of time to find a house she liked.

CHAPTER 29

He's so excited about the boat. It makes me happy to see him like that.

Mela knocked on the heavy wooden front door and stepped back. Amelie's house still looked the same as she remembered, down to the window boxes with the geraniums that seemed more Austrian Alps than coastal Maine. Mela faintly recalled that Meredith, Amelie's mom, had gone to Austria and returned fervently in love with the sturdy red flowers.

Amelie was still in her PJ's when she opened the door, a silky sleep mask pushed into her short curls. "Good morning!" Blinking, she stepped into the sunshine to hug Mela.

"Good morning. I picked up your newspaper from the driveway."

Amelie took it and tucked it under her arm. "Come on in. I slept in for the first time in ages, but at least I just made tea. Let me just run upstairs and get dressed."

She led the way into the living room full of cozy cottage sofas and throws and books. Mela set her bag on an overstuffed chair. "No need to hurry. If you like, we can go sit outside while you have your first cup."

Amelie struck a pose. "You don't mind my PJ's?"

"I love pink stripes. Don't ever wear anything else. Um. How's the bee sting?"

Amelie pushed back her sleeve to show Mela the lemon-sized swelling. "It hurts when I press on it. How's yours?"

"Mine is fine." Mela couldn't even remember exactly where it was. Somewhere on the shoulder. Inspecting the new hives, she'd stumbled and bumped one of the stacked towers. The bees had taken offense and chased Amelie and Mela off.

"I've never had a reaction to bee stings," Mela admitted sheepishly. "I'm sorry about yours. I brought you a gift to make up for it." Mela loosened the drawstring of her bag and pulled out a tube of ointment as well as a brand-new paperback novel. She handed both to her friend. "My sincere apologies. It will probably happen again."

Amelie laughed and took both. "You're forgiven." She opened the tube and rubbed the clear gel on her swelling. Waving her arm to dry the gel, she inspected the book cover. "Ooh, goody, a historical mystery. I don't know the author. Is she good?"

"Yes," Mela said. "She's very good indeed. It's all about Egyptian pyramids and walking mummies and the grumpy love of the archaeologist-detective's life. You'll adore it."

"Every time I get stung, I get a new book?"

"Why not? We both win." Mela winked. Amelie had enjoyed the field and the bees very much—until she'd gotten stung and they'd had to leave to find some ice. Luckily, the nearby dairy farm had a little ice cream stand and readily supplied a plastic bag full of ice cubes as well as massive portions of freshly churned strawberry ice cream in homemade waffle cones.

"Hmm." Amelie inspected her swelling.

"Kidding aside...if you'd like to come out again, I'll get a couple of full beekeeping suits," Mela said as she followed Amelie into the kitchen. "You'll get hot, but you'll be safe."

"I'd like that better." Amelie picked up a tray of sticky cinnamon buns smelling like a dream and led Mela onto the small patio.

They found Bennett outside in one of the comfy wicker chairs, dressed in slacks and a white button-down shirt. He was reading on his phone and had an empty teacup standing on the table beside him. When he saw Mela, he stood. "Good morning."

"Good morning, Bennett. I hope I don't disturb your morning peace." Mela looked at her friend, and Amelie sent an I-*know*-they'd-be-perfect-together vibe back.

"Not at all, I'm glad you're here. Mom, is the tea ready?"

"I just poured the water—and these rolls are right out of the oven, so make sure you come back out here and join us." Amelie smiled fondly at her offspring and set her tray on the table. "Sit down, Mela."

They sat, Amelie pulling her bare feet up. Bennett reappeared with the pot and served the tea.

Amelie took a sip, turned her face in the sun, and closed her eyes.

Mela smiled. "What's on your schedule today?"

Amelie opened one eye. "Not beekeeping, unless you already have that suit you were mentioning.

"I have to order it. Julie never even wore a veil. She just opened the hives and went right in. I can't remember ever seeing her react to stings either—maybe I inherited her immunity."

"Did you know that Pamela means honey? I think I read that somewhere."

"I didn't. Maybe that's why Julie picked it. I like it."

Amelie chose a sticky bun and bit into it. "To answer your question, I have a couple of clients later, and Bennett and I might look at places he could rent."

"Kimmie and Johanna are looking as well," Mela said. "Though they want to buy. Maybe Bennett should consider it as well—the market is exceptionally good."

Bennett sat back in his wicker chair. "But a policeman's salary doesn't easily buy a house at the coast, even in a buyer's market."

Mela didn't know whether he was serious. It wasn't any of her business, but shouldn't Amelie be swimming in money? Surely, she would help. "I have to tell you something. About Sunny." Mela cleared her throat. "Julie and Sunny might have been related."

Amelie let the bun sink. "What do you mean?"

Bennett frowned as if she'd just given him a case to solve.

"We started piecing it together last night. It seems my grandmother had a baby before she married, which means Julie had either a sister or, more likely, a half sister." Mela told the story again. It helped her too—every time she told the story, it became a little more real.

"No way," Amelie said. "Are you serious?"

"Kimmie ordered a couple of genetic test kits for us," Mela confirmed. "Then we'll know for sure. But I'm already certain from seeing how much Sunny and Julie looked alike as babies. Julie found a baby photo of Sunny in her mother's nightstand."

"Oh, I hope it's true because that would be wonderful," Amelie said. "Sunny needs a family in Bay Harbor. She has Peter, of course, but family is different."

"I'm going to ask Sunny to move in with me, I think."

"Are you?" Amelie nodded in agreement.

"I think Julie would have loved the idea of Sunny and me living in her blue house," Mela said. "So do I." She'd already considered asking Sunny to move in before the photo. With a few easy modifications, her house would be more comfortable to navigate than the upstairs motel room, and Sunny would have easy access to the patio and the view of the ocean she loved so much. "I'll ask her today. She can always say no."

"I think it's a lovely idea," Amelie said. "But run it by Peter too. Just so he's prepared when his perma-guest moves out all of a sudden. He doesn't have any family in town either. He and Sunny are close by now."

"I will," Mela said. "I do feel a bit bad snagging her for myself."

Amelie laughed. "He'll pretend it's just what he always wanted. We need to fill his motel with real guests. You have another son and daughter, don't you? Ask them to visit you sometime and bring their friends to stay at the motel."

Mela liked the thought of filling the old motel with friends and family. "Rob and I used to lure the kids with expensive vacations," Mela said. "That's over now. But at least Kimmie seems to have fallen in love with Bay Harbor." Sisley and Morris had always been harder to get. Sisley had her boyfriend, and Morris was performing or traveling.

"If you're discussing your children, of whom I'm one, I'm going to leave you to it," Bennett said. "I'll go on a quick walk down to the harbor and see if I can find a store that sells the Cape Bass Report." He left, taking a cinnamon bun with him and giving them a wave.

"I love him," Mela said when he was gone. "You did a great job, Amelie."

"It wasn't me." Amelie stood to toss the cold tea from their cups and refilled them. "You and the kids don't see each other often?" she asked. "Tell me about them. Are they as busy as Kimmie?"

"They're all very different from each other." Mela sipped, burning the tip of her tongue. She sucked in a cooling breath. "Very different. Sometimes I wonder how it happened, but I think they mostly just came out like that."

"Tell me about them. I know their names, but little else. Your son's name is Morris, right?"

Mela nodded. "He'll be twenty-five in August."

"Is he a concert pianist?"

"Yes, though it's early days yet. He plays jazz too, and he has a band. Or the band has him—however that works." Mela noted, somewhat startled, that she didn't know very much about her son anymore.

"My youngest is Sisley. She's twenty-one and taking a break from college. It seems she changes her mind about her major every other week. I think it's fine to look around, though I have my wobbly moments worrying about her."

"It'll all work out," Amelie reassured her. "I'm sure you and Rob put them on the right path."

"I would like to see them," Mela said suddenly. "I wonder whether I can talk them into coming this summer. They should know where I live now."

"Hey, I meant to ask... How did they take the news about the divorce?"

Mela pushed her cup away. "I can only say that they took it. Neither one has commented much. Morris asked if I was sure. Sisley just seemed distracted."

"Well, call them today!" Amelie stood. "Invite them to come see your house and see what they'll say."

CHAPTER 30

It was a horrible accident. But Sunny is finally free. She won't have any more bruises.

Mela stacked the cups and carried them into the kitchen while Amelie took the plates and the tray. She should call the kids.

Amelie put the plates in the sink and ran hot water over them. "I have to get ready for my first client. Are you going to do more beekeeping?"

"I think I'm going to call the kids, and then I'll pick up Sunny for lunch," Mela decided. "Kimmie is coming out to the bees with me later." She rinsed the teapot and wiped it dry. "Thank you for breakfast, Amelie. I'll see you later."

Out on the sun-drenched street, Mela remembered a bench overlooking a gentle sweep of rock pools down to the sea. When she got there, she pulled out her phone and dialed Sisley.

"Mom? Are you all right?"

"Yes, I am, Sis. I was thinking of you and thought I'd check in. How are you?"

"What's going on?" Her youngest sounded alarmed.

"Nothing, sweetheart. I'm just calling to see how you are."

"You never just call to see how I am, Mom."

Mela felt a pang of guilt. She did call, but not very often. "Maybe we can talk more often, baby. How are you?"

"I'm...okay," Sisley said. She sounded guarded.

Mela's eyebrows rose. "No better than okay?"

"Lars broke up with me. It just happened, Mom. I'm...I'm not in a good place right now. I feel alone." Her voice wavered.

"Oh no, I'm so sorry to hear that." Mela had never met Lars, but the relationship with the Norwegian student had been going on for—a year? A year and a half? Sisley had seemed happy with him, focusing entirely on her relationship. "Listen, sweetheart, I'll send you the address to my new place in Bay Harbor and money for a flight, okay? Come and stay with me for a while. You can catch up on sleep and sun and swimming. You are not alone. I love you. We all do."

Sisley sniffled. "I love you too, Mom. Is Dad there?"

"No, he's in New Hampshire," Mela reminded her gently. "Unless he's traveling, of course. You can go see him, too, if you would rather." Rob was a good man, but he wasn't the most nurturing when it came to his children's feelings. Mela held her breath, willing Sisley to come to Bay Harbor. The seaside town had a healing atmosphere that was already working on Kimmie.

Sisley cleared her throat. "No, I want to see you. Can you send me the ticket?"

"On its way!" Mela tried to keep the glee out of her voice, but—it had worked! It'd been months since Sisley had visited. There'd always been some excuse or other. In fact, Mela had started to think that it was Lars who didn't want to come visit and that he was keeping Sisley away from her family. Maybe it was no coincidence that as soon as Lars was gone, Sisley was able to come.

"Did you invite Morris too?" Sisley wanted to know.

"I'm going to call him as soon as I hang up," Mela promised.

There was a small pause. "Okay. I'll see you soon, Mom."

"I can't wait, sweetheart."

Sisley ended the call, and Mela sent money to her PayPal account with instructions to rent a car from the airport in Portland to Bay Harbor.

Then she called Morris and left a message on his voice mail. His phone was usually muted because he was either listening to music or playing it.

As soon as she put her phone down, it rang. "Morris?" she asked.

"Who is Morris?" Peter asked.

"Hello to you, too. Morris is my son."

"Oh. Oh. Hello. I was hoping to see you today."

"I'll stop by to pick up Sunny later. Are you at the motel?"

"Yes, I am. Mela—can we talk?"

Mela exhaled. They had to take care of whatever was developing between them, even if she didn't yet know what she wanted. She wasn't quite divorced yet, and it seemed too early to fall in love again. But she couldn't forget the small, special moments between them. She couldn't even forget the feel of his hand holding hers forty years ago. The memory of his lips brushing her forehead still lingered on her skin.

She inhaled and closed her eyes. "Yes, I think we should talk, Peter." She could start by telling him the names of her children...

"I look forward to it. Oh. Mela, one more thing."

She felt her heartbeat speed up. "Yes?"

"Did you take the blue truck by any chance? It's fine if you did."

Her eyes opened again. "I drove my car, remember?" He'd walked her to it the night before.

"I guess I wasn't focusing. On...that."

Mela had to smile. She hadn't been able to focus on anything else but their goodbye hug, either. "Is the truck gone?"

"It is. Have you seen Johanna? She's missing too. I can't read the phone number she put in the ledger."

Mela frowned. "Didn't she sleep at the motel?"

"I don't know. She didn't come down for breakfast, and Sunny said she didn't hear her move around. If she went for a midnight swim or a walk without telling anyone and the tide got her... I think I should find her to make sure she's all right."

"I'll call her." Mela felt her frown deepen. She ended the call and speed-dialed Johanna.

Johanna picked up immediately. "Yes?" The deep rumble in the background told Mela where her former assistant was. Or more precisely, what she was driving.

Relief smoothed Mela's forehead. "Hi, Johanna. Are you okay?"

"Yes. Oh, shoot. Did Peter notice the truck was missing?"

"He did. He doesn't mind; he's just worried you went for a midnight swim by yourself and got swept off your feet."

Johanna laughed. "No, I'm smarter than going into deep water at night. I'm actually on the way to your house. Are you at home?"

The laugh was reassuring. Mela checked the time. "I'll be home. What are you up to?"

"You'll see. I'll be there in half an hour." Johanna hung up.

Mela put her phone down. "What are you up to?" she whispered. Then she checked the time again and decided to use her half hour to pick up Sunny.

She quickly walked back from the harbor to the bistro where her car was parked, and then she drove to the motel.

"Mela!" Peter stepped out of the vehicle shed, blinking into the sun. His T-shirt was streaked with motor oil, and his hands were stained. "I'd have washed up if I'd known you'd come so quickly. I should try calling you more often." He smiled.

"I found Johanna. She has the truck and is on her way to my house. I wanted to pick up Sunny before she gets there."

"What is that girl up to?" Peter pulled out a rag from the back pocket of his jeans and wiped his hands. "Johanna, I mean."

"I have no idea," Mela admitted. "But I'm going to find out and also, make lunch for Sunny."

"Fantastic." He lifted an eyebrow. "That way I don't have to."

Mela smiled. "Peter, if it's all right with you, I'd like to ask Sunny to move in with me. I think it'd be easier on her hip if she doesn't have to navigate stairs, and she could do more on her own."

Peter jerked his arms up, pretending to thank the sky. "Finally!" he whisper-yelled. "I'm free!"

"Yeah, yeah." Mela had to laugh. "Just wait and see. You'll be sorry to lose her."

He let his arms drop and grinned. "Just kidding. Of course I'll miss her. I'll be over at your place all the time, cutting up her cheese and crackers."

Mela hesitated. This was when she should tell him that they should take it slow...that she wasn't divorced yet and needed time to heal. But how much time did they have? How much did she have to heal? And would she heal best alone?

She saw the light in his eyes dim, his shoulders square a little. She moistened her lip. "I'd like that," she said firmly. "I like you, Peter."

He came closer, so close she could smell the engine oil, the freshly washed shirt, the scent of his skin. For a moment, she thought he'd kiss her again. A real kiss, not a butterfly brush of lips that only left her wanting more.

"I know you do," he murmured, his eyes holding hers. He stuffed the rag back in his pocket, and then he reached out and cradled her head between his hands.

Mela couldn't speak. She couldn't think. He was too close.

Peter tilted her head to his, and when he spoke, his low voice made her spine tingle. "I've waited forty years for you, Mela. I don't want to wait a minute longer." He closed his eyes and lowered his head, slowly grazing his mouth along her jaw without allowing his lips to touch. His warm breath brushed the sensitive skin like a trailing feather.

Mela exhaled shakily.

"That's how I feel, too," he whispered into her ear. Then he straightened and let go.

Suddenly, it was easy.

Mela reached for his hand. The memory of Peter taking her hand when she'd needed him had slept inside her all these years.

She'd tried to recapture the feeling with her boyfriends, with Robert. And even though her marriage had been a good one until the end, there was a part of Mela that had been as deeply buried as her memories of Bay Harbor. Returning home had shaken her awake, and remembering Peter had shown her what she wanted.

Peter lifted her hand and kissed the tips of her fingers. “Sunny’s upstairs,” he said. “Do you need help bringing her down?”

Mela knew what she wanted, and now the pressure to make a decision was gone.

“The divorce is almost finalized,” she said when she could. “Peter, give me time to settle in. I want all of me to be there for you.” She smiled. “As for Sunny, I think I’m fine.”

Peter let his eyes graze down her body and back up to her face. The skin next to his eyes crinkled. “Yes, you are, Mela.” He left, walking past her to the reception and disappearing into the motel.

“Oh,” Mela whispered. She cast a glance over her shoulder, hoping nobody had seen her stand and stare after Peter like a transfixed teenager. Then she hurried up the stairs and along the balcony until she reached Sunny’s room, lifted her hand, and knocked.

“Hey, Sunny? It’s me, Mela.” She waited, pressing her hands against her flushed cheeks to cool them down.

“Sunny?” She knocked again.

Again, there was no response.

CHAPTER 31

I told him he couldn't take the girls out on the boat yet. It's not that I don't trust him, I do. But I first want to test it myself.

Mela pressed against the weathered wood, and the door to Sunny's room swung open. Her gaze flew over the empty bed and the deserted balcony.

She froze. Had Sunny accidentally... Hearing only a ringing in her ears, Mela hurried to the balcony and looked over the balustrade.

Nothing. Below lay the sunny garden. Nothing but green grass and the blue and pink pom pom blooms of the hydrangeas waiting for butterflies and bumblebees.

"Sunny?" She turned to go back inside when fingers curled around the privacy wall.

"I'm here. Mela? Is that you? Help me, honey. I can't get—"

Mela leaned around the half-wall and saw Sunny trying to squeeze past the chair Johanna had pushed onto the balcony. She laughed out loud with sheer relief.

"It's not funny, getting old," Sunny remarked dryly.

"No, of course not. Here." Mela came over and picked up the wedged-in chair, lifting it enough so that Sunny could pass.

"Oof. Thank you. I thought I'd have to call Peter."

Mela put the chair back and followed Sunny. Her aunt lowered herself carefully on the bistro chair and closed her eyes, exhausted.

"Why didn't you call Peter?" Mela asked.

Sunny opened her eyes again. "I didn't bring my phone. Besides, he'd be mad if he knew I went into Johanna's apartment. But I wanted to make sure she was okay. I'd not seen her, so..." She straightened defiantly. "I *told* him to go check on her. Skinny little thing like that could faint any moment."

Mela laughed. "Jo is a skinny little thing, but she's all muscle. I promise you the woman is three times as strong as you and me together."

"Oh good. But where is she? Did she find another place to stay?"

"She's on the way to my house. I came to see if you'd like to come as well. We can ask Johanna what she's up to because she's up to something."

"Oh. Yes, I'd like that." Sunny narrowed her eyes. "But you don't have to do it out of pity. Just because we might be related doesn't mean you have to care for me."

Mela rose and held out her hand. "It's not out of pity. It's not even that you are Julie's sister and my aunt. I just want to spend the day with you."

"Well, the... Don't mind if I do." Sunny took the hand and rose. "Oof."

"Did you have someone look at that hip of yours lately, Sunny?"

"Not in a while, though I do have old x-rays lying around somewhere."

Mela led her aunt inside. "We should see a doctor and have another look at your options."

"Well..." Sunny weaved her head.

"It's on me," Mela said. "Please don't worry about the money. I have enough for the two of us, I promise."

"I don't know," Sunny said, taking her purse from the hook on the door and leaning on Mela's arm as they left the room. "You save your money for your kids."

"There's enough to go around," Mela assured her. "I want you to enjoy your life more than I want to sit on my money." She smiled. "And I'm still looking for a beekeeping assistant. Maybe you can be it."

Sunny stopped by the stairs, taking an asthmatic breath. "Money aside, do you really think they could fix me?"

"Sure," Mela said. "I know several people who had hip replacements. It takes a while to heal, but if you're careful and do what the doctor says, you get your walking legs back."

"Don't build me up," Sunny said and started her arduous descent to the ground. "Or I'll take you up on it. If you can put me on the insurance, that is. You're not paying for the surgery out of pocket."

"I'll look into it right away," Mela promised. "Meanwhile, it might be helpful to lose a little weight," Mela said. "And find what doctors are close by."

They reached the bottom and slowly made their way to the car.

Mela helped Sunny into the passenger seat, and they drove to Seasweet Lane, where Sunny insisted on fixing iced peach tea while Mela boiled the lobsters she'd bought. She'd already made a buttery lemon sauce, a green salad, and a large dish of macaroni and cheese topped with roasted croutons. Mela had the patio table set and Sunny seated by the time she fished the lobsters from the steaming stockpot.

The sun was shining, the sky and sea were as blue as cornflowers washed clean after a rain, and the air smelled of sunscreen and salt.

"This is so beautiful; it makes my heart ache," Sunny said contentedly. Mela had stuffed her chair with pillows so the hip wouldn't bother her. "Don't you think? I only wished Julie could be here with us, all old and crotchety."

Mela wiped the condensation running down her iced tea glass with a napkin. "I don't think Julie would've ever turned crotchety. She was too sweet."

"Aw, you never know." Sunny sighed. "Why is it always the good ones who get taken?"

"It's the good ones who are missed most," Mela said gently. "But she's here with us. Sometimes, I can feel her presence as much as if she were standing beside me."

"You're just as sweet as she was. Here's to my little sister." Sunny lifted her peach tea, and Mela followed her example. "Here's to you, Mom," she whispered.

They drank. Mela was about to say she was going to give Johanna a call when the house door slammed shut.

"Mela? Are you here?" Johanna called out.

Mela stood. "We're on the patio!"

A second later, Johanna appeared. She looked tired but happy. "Hi! Oh, hi, Sunny." She plopped on a chair and pointed at Sunny's plate. "That looks delicious. I'm late because I stopped for a lobster roll and fries myself. It was so good."

Mela went to get the pitcher and poured Johanna a glass. "You have cobwebs in your hair," she remarked. "What in the name of everything have you been up to? We were worried."

Johanna put a hand to her heart. "Aww, were you?" She took a long, deep drink.

"Yes. We were," Sunny scolded. "I broke into your place just to check that you're okay." She coughed guiltily.

"Did you?" Johanna smiled at her. "You're the sweetest. And also, that's good because now we're quits. I broke into your place."

"Nah, I was in my room," Sunny said. "You broke into someone else's place."

The blue truck flashed through Mela's mind. She tucked her chin. "You *haven't*, Jo," she said. "Have you?"

Johanna grinned happily. "Yes. I broke into your other place last night, Sunny. The house by the landslide."

Sunny set her tea down hard enough to make a thump. An ice cube jumped the glass and slithered over the table to Mela, who dexterously flicked it into the flower bed. "It's too dangerous to play around that house. The whole thing could crash down the cliff any moment."

"The ground has had years to settle. I researched it before I went. There've been winter storms and rains since the landslide, and nothing has moved. Plus, I was roped and all that."

Mela narrowed her eyes. "Your rope would be no use at all if the house went down with you in the basement, Johanna. Promise me you're never going back in there. The county closed the area down for a very good reason."

"And yet," Johanna said, not promising anything, "it was perfectly fine. Not a wobble all night."

"You were in there the entire *night*?" Sunny looked like she was going to be sick. "I should call the police to lock you in for safekeeping."

"You should be happy instead of locking me up, Sunny. I was getting your things, at least as much as I could grab in a night. The truck is loaded with boxes." She grinned, unrepentant. "If you tell the police, they might confiscate all those fat photo albums I snagged. Wouldn't that be a pity?"

"Help me, Mela," Sunny said weakly. "I want my photos, but I don't want her to think she did well."

Mela shook her head, exasperated. "Don't do it again, Jo," she said. "It was a grand gesture, but imagine how Sunny would feel if something had happened to you. Or me. Or all the other people who truly care about you."

"So, do you want to know what's in the truck?" Johanna asked happily.

CHAPTER 32

I wish we could always be together, but I know she will grow up and live her own life. I hope it will be full of love and joy, even when I'm not with her anymore.

Johanna's yellow shirt was full of dust and dirt streaks, exactly like one would expect of a shirt after a day of moving boxes. "Because if you don't want it, let me know." She emptied her glass. "I'll bring it back right after I've had a swim."

Sunny's mouth opened, and then it closed. "I want it, Johanna," she said finally. "I want it so badly you have no idea. But I want you a whole lot more. Don't go back. I could never forgive myself if something happened to you. I'd rather blow up the place tomorrow, photos and everything."

"That's why I didn't tell you what I was planning," Johanna said. "I knew it was possible, but I also knew it wasn't a risk you were willing to take. But here I am, all fine and dandy, and you have at least some of your things back. So..." She shrugged. "It happened. And now we must move on."

"Thank you," Sunny said after a short pause. "But don't do it again."

"No," Johanna said. "I promise I won't. Look what I found in the bathroom, though." She pulled something from her pants pocket and set it on her palm. "I had to put it in the matchbox to keep it safe."

Sunny raised an eyebrow. "What is it?"

Johanna pushed the box open, and something splintered the light. "It's a diamond ring. Yours, I figured."

Sunny put a hand to her throat, and her eyes filled with tears. "I took it off the night before the landslide and forgot to put it on again." With trembling fingers, she picked up the ring. "Thank you, Johanna."

"So where do you want the boxes?" Johanna asked. "I have a whole truck full."

"We'll bring them in here," Mela offered. She cleared her throat. "Sunny, I was going to soften you up a little first, but I meant to ask if you want to move in with me."

Sunny closed her fingers over the ring. "Move in? Here?"

Mela nodded. "If you don't mind sleeping off the kitchen, we can turn the pantry into a small bedroom. That way, you don't have to climb stairs until your hip is fixed. When the stairs are easier, you can have your pick of the bedrooms upstairs. Even your sister's."

"Don't you want it for yourself?" Sunny's voice wavered as if she was going to cry.

Mela went to her aunt and hugged her. "I do, but I'd rather have you than the room."

The front door opened and fell shut again. A second later, Kimmie stormed onto the patio. Her cheeks were flushed with heat, and her eyes shone with excitement. "Mom! I found a house! It's so cute; I can't stand it!"

Slowly, Mela straightened. "You found a house? What do you mean?"

"I found one! I'm putting in a bid. The real estate agent is drawing the documents right now. It's a foreclosure, so it might take some time, but he said the local bank was eager to get rid of it."

"Oh, honey!" Mela hugged her daughter. "We're really going to be neighbors?"

"Yes! At least in the summers. I'm still going to be in the city to work." Kimmie hugged her back. "But I'm going to find someone to take care of the house when I'm gone. You don't have to worry about it." She spotted Sunny, who was quietly sitting in her chair. "Hi! So you're my great-aunt, then?"

Sunny tried to stand, but Kimmie was at her chair and hugging her before she could.

"I think so, child," Sunny said in a muffled voice. Mela couldn't see her face, but it sounded from her aunt's voice as if tears were flowing. "I'm so glad to meet you." She sniffled.

When Kimmie re-emerged, there was a sheen to her eyes, too. "I always wanted to have a great-aunt," she claimed. "I just didn't know it."

Mela breathed a sigh of relief. Kimmie could be reserved, but if she liked someone, she was all in. If Sunny was going to live here, having Kimmie on her side would make life much easier.

Kimmie rubbed the back of her hand over her eyes. "Mom, can I have some of the tea? I'm dying of thirst."

"I'd like another glass too," Johanna said. "I'll go get it."

"You have done enough, Jo. Sit down, you two." Mela left to get more iced tea.

As she pulled the pitcher from the fridge, the front door clicked open and closed again.

Pitcher in hand, she went into the living room to see who it was now. Peter? Amelie?

"Mom? It's me. I caught a flight an hour after you called." Sisley stood at the door, dressed in a T-shirt and loose denim overalls. Beside her was a suitcase, and she lowered another duffle bag. "I knocked, but I don't think anyone heard me."

"Sisley!" Mela couldn't think; she was so surprised. Not because her daughter had managed to get to Bay Harbor so quickly—she knew a lucky string of departing flights and punctual rides made it possible—but by the way her daughter looked.

Usually, Sisley was what Sunny would call a skinny little thing. More than anyone, she came after her slender grandmother.

But not now. Now she was—

Mela set the pitcher on the coffee table before she spilled anything. Her hand trembled that much. "Sisley, darling, are you *pregnant*?"

Sisley put a hand on her round belly. "Eight months to the day, Mom."

"And Lars..." Mela couldn't even put it together in her head.

Her youngest shook her head, sending her blond hair flying. "I'm here by myself." She slipped her hands into the pockets of her overalls, the way she'd done when she'd been a little girl, and tilted her head, uncertain. "Mom, I know you just moved here and all that. But do you think I—can I stay with you? I thought I could do it on my own, but I really want you."

The worried look in her daughter's eyes just about broke Mela's heart. How long had Sisley struggled before she'd asked? Mela strode to her girl and pulled her into her arms. Sisley felt foreign to hug, and she smelled of airport and travel as if she needed a good airing out.

"Of course you can, sweetheart," Mela said. "I always have room for you. Do you want to wash up or come outside and meet everyone? Or—" She needed to sit down. Right now. She grabbed the arm of a chair and lowered herself onto it.

"I'm sorry, Mom," Sisley said. "I wanted to tell you, but he said I had to keep it a secret or he'd leave me. I didn't know what to do. I felt so alone."

"You know what, Mela?" Sunny called happily from the patio. "I accept your offer and move in with you!"

"Great!" Mela called back. "Hang on, I'll be there in a second."

"Who's that?" Sisley tilted her head.

"That's my aunt. I think." Mela wanted to exhale, but instead of a steady stream of air, laughter suddenly burst from her.

For years and years, her life had been all about Rob and politics and to-do lists. She'd forgotten penciling in time for her feelings, her children's hearts, her forgotten friends, and her blue house. It all had gathered and risen like water, and the wave was finally breaking, sweeping her where she needed to be.

This was a new life. This was the life she wanted with all of her heart.

Mela stood, determined to make it the best one she could. Amelie had said 'When we're happy, we can make others happy.' It was time to fulfill that saying.

Mela put an arm around her daughter. Her flutters had gone, and she felt steady and calm, fully in charge. "We'll have to get ready for the baby. Is it a boy or a girl?"

"It's a little girl," Sisley said, resting her head on Mela's shoulder. "I'll show you the ultrasound photos. She's pretty cute." She sighed a sigh full of untold stories. "Mom, I know it wasn't supposed to be like this. I messed up really badly, and I almost can't think of anything but all the things I did wrong. I tried so hard, and in the end, Lars left anyway. But I love her. I love her..." She abruptly stopped speaking and swallowed.

"I love her too." Mela hugged her daughter fully, her eyes filling with tears of joy that she was granted another little girl in her family.

They stood for a while before Mela stirred. She wiped her eyes and smiled at her youngest. "Let's take a load off, darling. The worst is over. Now comes the good part; we'll make sure to make it the best."

Sisley met her eyes. "How do I start, Mom?"

"Let's start with a tall glass of iced peach tea and getting to know everyone," Mela said. "I promise that whatever you are, sweetheart, you are not alone."

Sisley nodded.

Mela hooked Sisley's arm under her own and took a deep breath. "Get ready for a surprise, everyone!"

Thank you so much for reading! Get ***Seaside Sunrise*** for more on families, friends, and neighbors as they take on old secrets and new beginnings!

The Bay Harbor Beach Series

Lose yourself in this riveting saga of old secrets and new beginnings as you walk cobble streets smelling of salt water taffy, browse quaint stores for swimsuits, and sample pies at the Beach Bistro!

Seaside Friends

Seaside Sunrise

Seaside Rumors

Seaside Ties

THE BEACH COVE SERIES

Old friends, new neighbors, and secrets by the sea abound in this riveting saga!

Maisie avoided coming to the small town of Beach Cove for a decade. Now in her early fifties, a desperate search brings her back to her old beach house, new neighbors, and the friends she left behind.

Beach Cove Home

Beach Cove Inn

Beach Cove Sisters

Beach Cove Secrets

About the Author

Nellie Brooks writes heartwarming women's fiction with great characters. Her books are set in Maine, where Nellie likes to hike along the coast and spend time on the beach. Visit www.nelliebrooks.com to subscribe to her newsletter and learn about upcoming books, releases, and sales. You can also find Nellie on Facebook and BookBub.

Made in United States
Orlando, FL
27 April 2023